EVERY TRICK IN

THE BOOK

EVERY TRICK IN THE BOOK

IAIN HOOD

RENARD PRESS

RENARD PRESS LTD

124 City Road
London EC1V 2NX
United Kingdom
info@renardpress.com
020 8050 2928
www.renardpress.com

Every Trick in the Book first published by Renard Press Ltd in 2022

Text © Iain Hood, 2022

Cover design by Will Dady

ISBN: 978-1-913724-92-4

9 8 7 6 5 4 3 2 1

This is a work of fiction. Any resemblance to actual persons, living or dead, is purely coincidental, or is used fictitiously.

Renard Press is proud to be a climate positive publisher, removing more carbon from the air than we emit and planting a small forest. For more information see renardpress.com/eco.

This book has been checked by an insensitivity reader, to ensure the insensitivity of opinions expressed.

EVERY TRICK IN

THE BOOK

Everything I'm about to tell really did happen, just not the way I'm telling you. And when I paint, I'm the narrator, you're the reader, and everyone plays their part.

Kirov Tzucanari
Notebooks

Former Commissioner of Police of the Metropolis,
Dame Cressida Dick

(at the time Assistant Commissioner
of Police of the Metropolis for
Specialist Operations)

1.1

On a first visit your eye couldn't help but roam over the tastefully muted colours of the walls, of the skirting boards, of the large rug in the wide, short and low-ceilinged hall. On one side you'd note deep drawers, in dark-painted medium-density fibreboard, with handles of dull chrome. Above these, paintings of the image of a horse, the *Waverley* ferry sailing 'doon the watter' of the Forth of Clyde and a lighthouse on Skye directs the eye to muslin voiles hanging on thin, white, dusty metal hooks, which would falteringly close only with a tug of the hands. You would see the rug and floorboards end and a terracotta tile floor begin, naked and buffed.

Now your eye would scan an open space of eight metres by three metres. To the right, in front of a disused chimney breast, would be two small armchairs of pristine white chenille and again medium-density fibreboard shelves holding ornaments carefully arranged and displayed. Over on the other wall there would be a small relief map of Scotland, too small to see the detail of from here. In front of you there would be a large, high-backed couch and a rough Bakhtiari Garden carpet on the floor, seemingly held in place by small white hooks like on the rail for the muslin voiles; two dark-red leather easy chairs, parallel to the couch; then a chunky set of mango-wood bookshelves in distressed white, neatly displaying books of all sorts: fiction and non-fiction; cooking and gardening; travel guides; a *World Atlas of Wine*; a *Larousse*; both old and new Vintage Classics, Pelicans;

paperbacks and hardbacks; old and new first editions. In front of you here in a recess, piled one on top of the other are old tape cassettes and CDs, a CD player and an amp with, it might seem, too many buttons and lights; and on the floor, propped up against a wall, a colourful canvas capturing the moment of fireworks going off above the Edinburgh Military Tattoo. In a blocked-off wall space of bare brick, a sill still running along the bottom, there would be a picture of an empty rural scene. You would see a 1928 architect's table in teak and a large metal stool, devoid of any drawing implements. Two mobile phones, seven various chargers, an uncountable tangle of in-ear headphones, a Samsung Galaxy Tab 7.0 and a Kindle DX International would sit on a shelf by the door. Below a window sits a square, tall set of free-standing shelves, painted a dull orange, holding sparsely spaced ceramic ornaments, to the side of a circular iroko worktop with a stainless-steel mounting and high stand, with four leather-topped stools arranged around it, bringing the eye again to the muslin voiles.

Colours of chestnut, reds, sky and baby blues – deep and rich, sometimes incongruous, almost seeming thrown together – would prevail, with dark hues creeping in elsewhere – a Joan Miró-inspired fabric pattern here, the colour-matched red-, orange- and blue-spined books there. At night, a space that is too dark and low-lit; in the morning and afternoon the windows of the Victorian shell of the house cause revealing shafts of unusual light. And in the summer, this effect – on ornaments, CD spines, high iroko worktop and stools, glints from the stain-less steel, small pools of light, and thrown shadows on the floors and walls, the marble kitchen worktops, thin muslin, stainless steel, chenille – would make this seem like the beautiful life, the Sunday supplement life.

1.2

At last we reach the next room, which would again have wooden floorboards and rugs. A French queen-size would be here, near the door, and at each side, low and wide bedside cabinets with a comb on one and a watch and ring-holder holding three rings on the other, alarm clocks and small lamps on both, and then books lying here and there. Along one wall, freshly green-painted medium-density fibreboard doors would be built in, and a leather Eames recliner would be in front and just to the side of these. In the en suite you would see light dressing gowns; chrome fittings; our reflections – those people who are us staring back at us through a small, wall-mounted looking-glass. There'd be a Braun electric shaver and separate beard trimmer; toothbrushes; perfumes; deodorants; shampoos; conditioners; shower gels; bath gels; handwash and body washes; hair waxes and beard waxes. Simple emulsion whitewash and white egg-shell skirting and woodwork; everywhere white Egyptian cotton for towels and sheets and duvet. Back in the room, on a set of shelves, sits a large sphere light, an old tape cassette-radio player and a Kindle 1. The bed's headboard is solid, padded and plaid patterned. Light floods in from the street, and shadows are forming and lengthening. Under the bed are dust and books and a few forgotten things, and there in the en suite an unassuming, short, wide, colourful painting of a fish somehow seems too prosaic, informal and imperfect.

1.3

The next room is mostly empty. There are shelves, but these seem to serve no purpose. There are a few postcards – Susan

Alison MacLeod's *The Mythopoeia of Christ*, a detail from *Christ of Saint John of the Cross*, one of Escher's never-ending staircases, a portrait by Jeremy Andrews, a Kandinsky sketch, a sepia-tint photograph of boys in Glasgow by Oscar Marzaroli, Jenners in Edinburgh, J.B. Yeats' portrait of W.B. Yeats – Sellotaped or Blu-Tacked to the wall. Far off to the right is a short plastic set of drawers for holding stationery with a melted LP record moulded into a bowl shape on top next to an empty square plain white plastic lidded container. In front of a large window there's a low-slung sofa. Yet the feeling of emptiness predominates. No objects that give away the purpose or function of this room. A desktop computer is present, but it is on the exposed floorboard floor, keyboard and mouse stacked up against the monitor, gathering dust. There's a wide chair, right here in front of us, but you couldn't sit down on it, as it is stacked high with patterned pillows and throws, designs by Miró, Mondrian, Kandinsky, Klee, Picasso, Matisse. Other plastic objects seem to have form but no function: art objects; perhaps the unrecognisable out-of-context bits and pieces of large- and medium-sized children's toys. Upstairs are the children's bedrooms and another bathroom. A lovely house, a pleasant home.

1.4

The beautiful life, the Sunday supplement life. A simple life, gratifying, satisfying. Deliveries of takeaways when cooking in the cramped, dark galley kitchenette, where there's never enough storage or worktop space, could not be faced. In late June, in the evenings, is when the house is most alive.

1.5

After the school run they would potter and dawdle, smoking at the back door past the kitchen, or in the back yard. They would work from home for a while, then eat at home or go out for something to eat at a coffee shop, usually the independent one, but Starbucks when the independent one was closed.

Always neat but always informal, comfortable, liveable. It was just the way they lived, comfortably, creatively, thoughtfully. They would be on their laptops, listening to CDs, or just chatting quietly to each other. Dinner would be after the kids had eaten in front of their screens, having no interest, now, in sitting down with them. Sometimes they would all go out for pizza together.

A life like this could go on undisturbed, always neat, always comfortable, Sunday supplement photogenic, always beautiful, as though this life were made for them. Of course, they could walk away at any point, sell up and move anywhere, travel the world for a year or two, live near the beach in Costa Rica, perhaps, or visit Machu Picchu: their own family gap year. Anything would be possible. Free and in control; comfortable to go, comfortable to stay. A simple, beautiful life.

1.6

But if you were given more time to look around, having been deflected from the upper floor, the girls' domain, closer inspection in the hall, behind the front door, would reveal the unruly pile of posters, leaflets and placards – most, if not all, of which have the word, or perhaps words, ORGAN:EYES somewhere. Professionally-printed placards reading ORGAN:EYES THE EYES OF THE WORLD ARE ON YOU; an amateur placard in a child's painted hand reading ORGANEYES OUR EYES ARE WATCHING; ORGAN:EYES WE WATCH, WE SEE; SCRUTINEYES PARLIAMENT; and again, a child's painted script on a placard reading ORGANEYES WE ARWE WATCHING! THE WORlD IS WATCHING! Repeated often, a diagrammatic faceless head with index and middle fingers of a schematic right hand pointing one finger at each place where eyes should be, then the same faceless head with index and middle fingers pointing at the viewer of the image.

And going along the bookshelves slowly, methodically, you would notice the mixed and eclectic reading, though you would also notice the preponderance of certain books, due to the number by one author: here, Anthony Burgess and Joseph Conrad; there, Yukio Mishima, Flann O'Brien, Georges Perec and Anne Rice; here, books by or about Trotsky, Lenin, Stalin, Voltaire, Orwell; there, books by Dr Seuss, Hergé, Lewis Carroll, Mark Twain and Jack London; higher up, books by Hugh MacDiarmid, Lewis Grassic Gibbon and the Ossian texts; higher up still, the novels in translation of Romain Gary and Émile Ajar; on a shelf to themselves, books by Pablo Neruda and Tristan Tzara and Tom Stoppard; and then, lying off the shelves, casually tossed under a chair or elsewhere, books by John le Carré, Elena Ferrante, Richard Bachman, Woody Allen. A pattern would be emerging.

1 . 7

How happy they would be. People like many others. Normal people doing normal things normally. Or, rather, no one's normal – normal's not the right word. Natural. Natural people doing natural things naturally. Natural people, people at ease in their environment, their world, people at home in their own skins. People who know who they are. Their north London home at this time in the evening, on the 24th of June, the lazing informality of bare feet or sloppily falling apart slippers they wear at home. A woman and a girl in the main bedroom, the woman lying up in bed, legs slipped into the turned-down bedspread and quilt, reading her Kindle, Elena Ferrante, the girl across the foot of the bed, lying on her stomach, her legs swaying half time in the air to the music coming from her iPad through pink headphones into her ears, Sugababes.

Through at the dining table, a long oblong of rough-hewn laminate elm atop a repurposed IKEA frame, a young woman sits in the pool of light from a lowered long-wired, circular, brown ceiling lampshade, wearing glasses, her hair tied high at the back, doing her homework, the American Revolution, the man leaning over and into the pool of light to see what she's stuck on as she says that, no, it's not this she was asking about.

The man straightens and expresses an acknowledgement of his lack of understanding. The young woman twists and gets comfortable with her arm over the back of the chair and says, no, it was what one of her teachers was saying today about sub-atomic particles, and she makes clear that it's not homework. The man takes a deep breath and repeats his realisation he doesn't really know what the young woman means.

The young woman says that she doesn't really get it.

The man asks her what she doesn't understand. He walks round to a chair across from the young woman, who repeats what her teacher was saying, that down at a subatomic level, well, like there's protons and neutrons and electrons, right? The man questions whether this isn't atomic level.

With a slight sarcasm in her teenage voice, the young woman says that, yes, right, this is spot on, but even at that level we know mostly it's like fresh air. Not fresh air, but you know what she means: vacuum − nothing between these teeny particles, and electrons especially, just flying around in nothing, mostly nothing, oceans of nothing in comparison to the teeny, tiny boat on the ocean that the electrons are.

The man tells her that this is a nice image, a very good image.

The young woman thanks him. Was that sarcasm, the slightest of slightest hints, too? Then she continues that the teacher was saying today that at the subatomic level there are even tinier component parts of protons and neutrons and electrons, particles literally insanely small in vast, vast galaxy-sized spaces of vacuum, literally nothingness.

The man says that he's hanging on in there. So, the young woman continues, at this quantum level, it's insane, we are basically vacuum with these teeny, tiny, literally… she seems unsure what. The man asks what it is that's bothering the young woman about all this.

The young woman says, further to these concerns, that at a sub-quantum level particles just come into existence and then disappear. She sounds alarmed. The man mentions the Large Hadron Collider.

The young woman says that the teacher said that we can't be sure where anything is or whether it's there or not. The man mentions the Uncertainty Principle, with a level of uncertainty, you would have to say. The young woman thinks he is right in mentioning it, though. Then the man says solicitously that these facts, these data, such as they are, seem to be bothering the young woman.

She lifts her left arm and slaps it with her right hand and says something about the point she's making being self-evident. Look, the man knows to wait. He knows this young woman, how revelation works for her. She slaps lightly again and repeats herself, saying that she literally *feels* solid, but that she's not. At a quantum level she doesn't know where anything is. How can she feel *solid*? It's barely there. There's nothing there.

The man is smiling and says something reassuring, calls her 'kid', reassures her that the facts of life will just blow her mind sometimes. His tone is mocking. The young woman sits still, open-mouthed. And the man says that the facts will literally blow a gasket in her mind at some point.

She says that she just doesn't get it, looking down at her unbelievable arm.

1.8

In a kitchen drawer, a letter from the Right Honourable Emily Thornberry MP and their marriage certificate, which is addressed to Mr & Mrs Paul Dorian, 18 Moon Street, Apt. 18, London, United Kingdom, N1 0QU and says 'THE CITY OF NEW YORK, OFFICE OF THE CITY CLERK, MARRIAGE LICENSE BUREAU, License Number,' and the licence number, 'Certificate of Marriage Registration, This Is To Certify That Paul Dorian residing at 18 Moon Street, Apt. 18, London, United Kingdom, N1 0QU born on 03/10/1964 at Glasgow, United Kingdom and Julia Smith residing at 18 Moon Street, Apt. 18, London, UNITED KINGDOM, N1 0QU born on 01/27/1966 at Manchester, United Kingdom Were Married on 03/10/2005 at Office of the City Clerk, 1 Centre Street, NYC, NY 10007 as shown by the duly registered license and certificate of marriage of said persons on file in this office. CERTIFIED THIS DATE AT THE CITY CLERK'S OFFICE Manhattan NY, March 11, 2005. PLEASE NOTE: Facsimile Signature and seal are printed pursuant to Section 11-A, Domestic Relations Law of New York.' Then the seal, then the signature of Victor L. Robles, then, 'Victor L. Robles, City Clerk of the City of New York.' Then there's all the paperwork from this young woman's baby months, toddler years and early childhood, noting that she didn't get immunised for MMR, and she developed measles at age five just as the second kid was born. She developed pneumonia, was hospitalised in Edinburgh, the Western Infirmary, and then the Royal Hospital

9

for Sick Children. The paperwork for a second child, a young girl now, seems to be missing from the drawer; perhaps it has never quite made it to this archive status and it is in some technically live file, that discarded Cath Kidston bag, under the stairs. The man now kicks off his shoes, his sensible pair of black Loake Actons, the ones he wears to his job in the charity. Not the Docs and Converse of the life side of his work/life balance that sit amongst the posters and placards behind the front door. A lanyard lying by his side tells us the charity combats homelessness. Back through in the bedroom, the woman receives a text from a colleague, which reads, 'All OK with thedoc/policy leaving office now FINALLY.' Her lanyard, lying on the dressing table of the parents' bedroom, notes her work is with a campaign group for rape crisis and domestic violence services.

It's about to be eight o'clock and the Channel 4 News has just ended. The woman has moved upstairs to her ten-year-old daughter's bedroom and has fallen asleep in her bed beside her, a brush still in her hand. She was about to brush or had been brushing out her daughter's long hair. By the look of her, she is wiped out; like it has been a long week and she's still unwinding. The man and his fifteen-year-old daughter, having given up on her homework, are sitting on the couch, curled up together. He asks whether she wants to listen to some Beefheart. She gives him *the teenage look of death*. Now they're watching television and chatting about subatomic particles. She asks the man whether he thinks he understands it. He looks like he's thinking of the best way to put it. Then he says that people don't like indeterminacy, and gives the example of that thing that happened a while back in the Met Police, where you could be clean-shaven or have a beard, but you couldn't be seen to be just unshaven.

The fifteen-year-old daughter quizzically questions him and tells him that he's always on about the police. The man says that he simply means that a copper who looks, you know, scruffy, couldn't be bothered, just is perceived to have no authority.

Clean, fine. Beard, fine. Authority. Anything else, then it just seems to him, this man, that then the police officer has no authority…

The fifteen-year-old daughter sounds exasperated and asks the man what he's talking about. She says that he's obsessed sometimes. He replies that, well, you've got to know what side you're on. Who the enemy is. He's just saying, in transition… She says she was talking about particles. And the man says something along the lines of, if we are catching it correctly, that well, yeah, at a subatomic level, they say, don't they, that we're only approximations of ourselves.

The fifteen-year-old daughter expresses both exasperation and thoughtfulness in a pause and tells him that, yes, that sounds about right.

The father leans forward and shows his daughter a card trick, but she's not that impressed, questions what tricks are, anyway. She gathers herself together, saying she's ready to go to bed, turns and walks to the stairs, trailing a blanket behind her.

The house cools down. The mother wakens in her younger daughter's bed and makes her way downstairs to where the father is asleep in their bed. Then you can hear the older daughter tiptoeing through to the younger daughter's bedroom, and there's the sound of their voices, talking into the night.

1.9

On a Tuesday this man, the father, has nothing to do in the afternoon and wanders away from the café where he was having lunch, not far along Upper Street and up a cul de sac and into a pub. It's his usual routine when he isn't meeting her, the mother, his wife, to walk home. This happens about once a week. He opens the door into the pub and looks surprised at the number of people for a Tuesday, for two o'clock in the afternoon. He scans the room.

Two men and two women at a table finishing off a pub meal; a group of three men at the bar, all quietly staring at their mobile phones; a group of five men, site workers, apparently finished for the day, down the end of the bar, laughing uproariously; the young woman sitting by herself over by the window, a flash of blonde hair and scarlet lipstick, one glass; a group of women, one, two, three… six of them around a table near the back room, talking. He scans back, the women, the woman, the laughers, the quiet ones, the two couples. Then he sees the woman by the window is smiling at him. He looks away and moves up to the bar between the two groups of men and orders a beer, taking his time, checking his change. Then, as he turns to sit somewhere, he's able to look past her again, and again she's looking straight at him, smiling, and she lifts the glass of white wine to her lips. When he sits at a table near the door the couples are between them, finishing their lunch, last mouthfuls of wine, last gulps of coffee. The father and husband looks down at his mobile phone and scrolls down through the headlines of the *Guardian*, then scrolls through them again; then we see shadows move and he looks up. The couples are leaving, and behind them comes the young woman, heading for the bar with her wine glass in hand. He looks down to scroll through the *Guardian* one more time. There's the smell of fresh cleanness and only a hint of perfume. As she passes, the young woman tilts her head to catch his attention. 'Hi,' she says.

'Yeah, hi,' he says. Then he looks down into his pint as he takes a mouthful. Immediately he takes another mouthful, looking around himself then down to his phone. When he looks up and around again the young woman is back sitting by the window, another glass of white wine on her table. She takes a drink, then another, then she stands and walks back over to the bar, and leans forward to say something to the barman, on tiptoe, her heels rising above her shoes, and her skirt riding up the back of her knees. He looks away, out of the window, at the laughers at the bar who have burst into another uproarious laugh and are shouting. He glances at the young woman as she turns and looks back down at his phone. Shadows change again. 'Hi,' she says.

The father, the husband, this man, looks up. 'Hi,' he says.

'You're Paul, aren't you? Paul Dorian?' she says.

'Yes,' he says. 'And you're... You're... I'm really sorry, I don't seem to remember... how we met.'

'Can I sit down?' she says.

'Sit? I mean... Yes, of course,' he says.

'Thanks,' she says, smiling, placing her glass of white wine in front of her.

This man, his name *is* Paul*, smiles back at her, watches as she takes a sip of wine. After a few moments he relaxes back into his chair and says, 'Is it through work... I know you? You know me?'

'What kind of work do you do?' she asks.

'So, not that, ha, hey?' he says nervously. 'Sorry, I didn't catch your—'

'No, I mean I was wondering what work you do,' the young woman says.

'Oh, right, um,' Paul says, 'I work for a charity. Homelessness.'

'Anything else?' she asks.

'Oh, you think it might be... We might know each other through the other work I do?' he says.

'Maybe,' she says, 'you never know. I'd certainly like to hear about it.'

'You would?' he laughs. 'You'd be about the only one.'

'Really? You think so?' she says. 'I'd say your *other* work is far more interesting, wouldn't you?'

Paul has been about to take a mouthful of his pint, smiling, watching her red lips. Again, the smell of the lightest of light touches of perfume. The young woman flicks her hair and then settles a strand in place behind her left ear.

'Don't you think your other work would attract media attention?' she says.

Paul hesitates. He sniffs and looks quizzical. Then he says, 'The media? Sorry, what's your… Do you know Stewart? It's just we're in such an early stage of… the project.'

The young woman is looking straight at Paul, almost staring straight into his eyes. He shifts in his chair. 'Oh,' she says, 'that's what you call it, is it? The project?'

'I mean, I… Yeah. I mean, no. It just is a project. It's not *The Project*, like that's its name,' Paul says. 'Are you sure—'

'No, not *the* project, I see,' she says. She lifts her glass of wine to her lips but then seems to place it back on the table without having actually drunk any wine. 'Or operation?' she adds.

'Are you…' Paul looks lost. He hesitates again, lifts his pint to his mouth and throws beer to the back of his throat. 'I'm not sure we're talking about the same thing.'

'Oh?' the young woman says, casual as you like. She looks him up and down. 'Maybe not. But you are Paul Dorian?'

Paul smiles as he holds his pint glass in mid-air, yet again frozen in the moment. 'So, you've heard about the label?' he says.

'Label?' she says.

'Well, yeah, the People's Republic of Rock and Roll,' he says. 'I mean, that's your interest, right? You know I'm involved in the setting-up of a record label? For… blues music. You knew that?'

'That's your other work?' the young woman says.

'Yeah. I mean, what else…?' Paul says.

She sits back in her chair. Something has changed in her, the look of her. Paul looks up and out of the window. It has begun to drizzle out in the street. The smell of her can't any longer hide the smell of a stale pub on a drizzly afternoon, the sickening hoppy sweetness of his beer gone warm, her wine a vinegary wersh. He drops his head and his eyebrows lower. His shoulders hunch and he stares at his phone. 'I'm sure now,' he says, 'I don't know what you're talking about.'

'I think you do,' she says.

14

'Who are you from? What media? Who are you? What's your name?' he says.

'I'm working freelance on this,' she says. 'But I'll probably try for the *Independent* or the *Guardian*. Those are the ones that have been taking an interest. Maybe the *Telegraph*. Come on, you knew this was coming, surely, after Mark?'

'How did you get to me?' Paul says.

'Well, now,' she says, 'that would be telling. That *is* telling.'

'You've got the wrong information,' he says. Then he looks around himself. 'I don't know what you think—'

She throws her hair back. 'We can play games if you want. Or not. I know what I just saw in your face. It tells me I'm sitting with a man who is in the police—'

'Slow down, for Christ's sake,' Paul says.

'You're really rattled,' the young woman says. She looks surprised at her ability to do this to him, and she's smiling, her eyebrows raised.

'Just… give me time to *think*,' this charity worker, this husband, this father, this man called Paul says.

'Sure. Here, take this,' she says, and she fumbles and pulls a scrap of paper with numbers on it from the inside pocket of her coat. 'And if you're thinking how you're going to explain everything to me…' She dips in and pulls her hand from her pocket again and her hand is on the table then gone, back in her pocket. And there's an Olympus digital voice recorder sitting on the table, but it has materialised and sits still as though it had nothing to do with her hand. It was a neat trick, an impressive sleight of hand all round.

'Not here,' Paul hisses. 'Jesus.'

'I don't mind where,' she says, reaching to switch on the voice recorder between them. 'Do you want to tell me about the woman? And about your own wife?' she says.

'My case isn't like the others, the other one,' Paul says. 'You've got this all wrong.'

'Oh? How?' the young woman says.

'There is no wife. I mean, there is a wife,' he says, 'but that's the woman I live with. She is actually my wife... I mean, the other's just... My wife and me, we've been together for twenty-odd years... You have to understand. We have children. You have to understand. Nothing you think you know is... correct. And you're going to have to leave us alone.'

'Or else?' she says. For a moment what Paul appears to be doing is looking from his phone to his pint, to the door and scanning the room. He twitches.

'That makes it worse. This all... the wife, the kids... all makes it worse,' the young woman says.

1.10

['Look, I tried...' Paul says. Then he is up and, 'Actually, no. I have nothing to say to you,' he says. Then her wine tips towards her and she grabs for the glass as he lightly shoves the table and, before you know it, he's disappeared out of the door.]

1.11

Now we see Paul outside his daughter's school, ███████████, waiting to collect his eldest and walk to the other school, ██████████████████, to pick up his younger daughter. When she sees him, she says, 'You know you can pick her up first.' She means her younger sister.

'Am I embarrassing you?' Paul says.

'I don't care about that,' she says.

'It's on the way to pick up Soph,' Paul says. (Her name is Sophie.* Soph to him. Very emphatically Sophie to everyone else.)

'You've got that look on your face,' his daughter says as they begin to walk along.

'Yeah, probably,' he says.

'Is it about that thing you said to me?' she says.

'What thing?' he says.

'The thing. Last year. You know,' she says.

'What?' Paul says. 'No. No. Not that.'

'It's just, I am ready, if, like you said, we had to move out from...' she says.

'No. No. Don't feel unsettled. I was in a... I was in a funny place back then. Things were up in the air between me and your mum. But that's all sorted now,' Paul says.

When the three of them get home, Paul tells the girls that they can watch or listen to whatever they like on the computer or television, as long as they wear earphones. Both of them wander off. Paul goes into the downstairs toilet and settles himself on the seat. He takes a deep breath, then stands and stretches up to an exposed beam which enters the wall leaving a small hole in the plaster above it. Taking a mobile phone out of this hole he settles himself back on the toilet seat. Another deep breath. Then he dials. 'I need to come in,' he says when he gets a response.

'How?' says the voice.

'Where's the boss?' Paul says.

'Which one?'

'The guv'nor,' Paul says.

'Scotland Yard.'

'There, then,' Paul says.

'You are joking, aren't you?'

'I need to see the big boss *now*,' Paul says.

'Aye. Naw. We're not going to blow everything by you running shitting yourself into the nest, now, are we? What's up, anyway?'

'Don't you read the papers?' Paul says.

'That's not going to happen to you, for Christ's sake. That numpty's investigations only go back a few years. You're, what, twenty years in? More than that? Who could spot you? It would have happened already.'

'That's what you say, but I have been spotted,' Paul says. 'A Nosey just sat down across from me in the pub and told me she knew who I was. What I was. Am.'

'Shite.'

There's a long pause.

'Are you still there?' Paul says.

'Shite.'

'Yeah, I know. Do I come in?' Paul says.

Another pause.

'Naw, we come to you first.'

'The big boss? The guv'nor? Or Fabius?' Paul says.

'Talk sense. We do it in stages. Fuck's sake. Don't blow this.'

'She said my years under made it worse. I suddenly saw it all from that perspective,' Paul says.

'Don't lose your nut. Just fucking… Right, this call is ended. I'll phone you back on this number in twenty… naw, ten minutes. Right?'

Another pause.

'Right?'

'Right, yeah, right,' Paul says.

'Sit tight. Remember, if we're panicking, they're winning.'

'What, fourteen ex-hippies, ten students, four trustafarians and two dogs on string?' Paul says.

'No them. You know who. The newspapers. And the others. Sit tight.'

'Right,' Paul says. 'Do something about this.' But the contact has already disappeared from his screen. There's a call back. Paul is still sitting in his downstairs toilet. He stares for a second at a fuzzy object when the mobile starts vibrating. In the early evening, before his wife – her name is Julia* – gets home, he tells his eldest daughter – her name is Olivia* (Liv to everyone) – that he's going to take a walk 'for some fresh air'. He says he won't be long to his younger daughter. There's a meeting at his local park. Paul talks fast to a colleague.

1.12

The next day Paul tells his wife that the label is going to fill up his whole day. He takes the Tube to Embankment (cameras 2, 12, 7B, 42, 1, 13, 9A, 7BC, 8FD, 72, 4, 6, #3, 7, 14, 12, 6, 9, 6YG, 27, A, B, 5, 1, 4, 7, 4, 3, 5, 2, 27, 5A, 7B, Front, Side, Back, 5, 13, 25, Backgate, 12, 4, 6, #9, #7, #1, f, ftdr, 4, 6, 8, 7), walks until he's past Victoria Coach Station (cameras FE, SE, BE, 6, 31, 22, 1, 3, 2, 1, FRONTGATE, 6, 5, 1, 3, 8, 6, 23, 13, 1, AB, CB, #5, #4, 2, 6, 3), takes the Tube to Piccadilly Circus (cameras 1, 4, No4, No3, No2, 3, 5, J, K, L, 2, 3, 7, 9, 3, X, XI, 4, SE, S, SW, 44, 32, 6), then loses himself in the crowd for a while before leaving the station. He walks to Scotland Yard (cameras Sideent, Backent1, Backent2, 3, 4, 2, 5, 1, 4, 6, 2, 7f, 7e, 7d), to a gate (a sign: Camera Enforcement In Operation, PIN numbered and ID card shown) and then a back door (cameras ▮▮▮▮▮▮▮▮▮▮▮▮▮▮). After he pushes the buzzer and enters after a response, he walks along a long corridor (cameras ▮▮▮▮▮▮), up three flights of stairs (cameras ▮▮▮▮▮), along another long corridor (cameras ▮▮▮▮▮▮), around a corner, then a short corridor (cameras ▮▮▮▮▮▮) and into a small, anonymous room which has a window into the corridor but no window to the outside world (camera ▮▮▮). The guv'nor is sitting across a table from him. He signals for Paul to sit in a plastic chair in front of him.

'Plush,' Paul says, looking around himself.

'I'm a busy man and I don't mess about. What the fuck are you doing here, Paul?' the guv'nor says.

'Well, I've said…' Paul says.

Nothing from the guv'nor.

'I've been spotted,' Paul says. 'Some freelancer female Nosey. She came up to me in a pub.'

'Oh?'

'You don't think that's a shitter?' Paul says. 'After Mark…'

'*Mark*. Jesus Christ Almighty. So what? Did it stop operations?'

'Yeah, I get that,' says Paul. 'But the impact…'

'There was no discernible impact.'

'No impact?' Paul says.

'It didn't stop operations. They go on. We put two more in, as a matter of fact.'

Paul's brow creases. His hands raise. 'I don't mean on the fucking operation,' he says. 'I mean *on Mark*. I mean *on me*. My *wife*. My *kids*. Don't you get what's going on here?'

'What did she say to you?'

'What? Uh, she said she knows…' Paul says.

'Stick to reporting procedure, please, fuckwit. Mock Jock,' the guv'nor says.

'She walked over,' Paul says, 'she, um, says hello, can she sit down. She names me, makes like she knows me…'

'*Names* you?'

'Yeah,' Paul says.

'She names *you*?' The guv'nor is pointing at Paul.

'Well, my deadkid, she names me in that life,' Paul says. 'You know, Paul Dorian.'

The guv'nor sits back in his seat.

'You can't think… It's not like… I mean…' Paul mumbles.

'A freelancer? Chasing down some fantasy she has? Some female Nosey with a butt plug up her arse about women being exploited? And all she knows is your deadkid? This is… fucking nothing, fuckwit.'

Paul's hands are dropping from in front of him. He looks breathless. He's open-mouthed. 'But…'

'Buttplug, mate. She knows tit-all. If she did she'd be with some paper, all backed up and ready to roll with something. She knows *something*. OK. That's irritating. Fucking proof? Fucking good lead? Nothing.'

'I just thought,' Paul starts, stops. 'I just think—'

'Next time you're in here, and I mean on pain of death, fuckwit, it's for reports – *on* something – or for lessons. Got me?'

'I...' Paul grinds to a halt on.

'Right. Good. Let's not waste this completely on bitch bleating.' Just at this moment, Fabius walks past the internal window in the corridor outside the room. The guv'nor says, 'I'm calling the sarge in. Beefheart pop quiz.'

'Not now. Jesus,' says Paul, watching Fabius walk on up the corridor.

'Aye now. You need to focus. And focus on what's fucking important here. You're Paul Dorian. You work for a homeless charity, but a lot of your time is taken up trying to set up a blues music label. Blues. Alternative blues. Bands influenced by Captain Beefheart. You're a big, big fan. This is who you are. Do you fucking understand, you fucking lefty lentil-muncher? Aye now.'

'OK. OK,' Paul says.

The guv'nor is looking at him.

'I'm saying OK. I get it,' Paul says. 'I'm ready.'

'Take it easy, Paul, you know?' the guv'nor says, turning from him.

1.13

The floor of the room is bare concrete painted a faint grey colour. Sunlight comes from somewhere, a window high up in the corridor, a squeezed rectangle much longer than it is high. When the sarge arrives, he's wearing full dress uniform, though no cap or helmet. 'How's tricks, Paul? We'll get started, shall we?' the sarge says.

Paul lifts his arms in resignation. 'Don't you want me to do it first?' he says.

'On you go, then,' the sarge says.

Paul pulls a deck of cards out of his pocket and shuffles them, professional-croupier style, a ripple then a bridge. He throws three cards face down on the table. The sarge picks one. Paul says, 'Four of diamonds.' The sarge turns it over and it is the four of diamonds.

'Every fucking time,' the sarge says. 'How's it done? Come on, tell me this time.'

'Nah, that would be telling.'

'OK,' the sarge says. 'Down to business, eh? Masterpiece?'

'*Trout Mask Replica*,' Paul says.

'Good. Why were the record company surprised by *Safe as Milk*?'

'The band had gone avant-garde,' Paul says. 'Record company thought they were signing a diddy wah diddy blues band equivalent of the British invasion, Rolling Stones, that sort of thing.'

'Good. Name the record company.'

'Um. Buddha?' Paul says.

'No, no "Um, Buddha?" It was Buddha. Any Beefhead kens that. What is up with you? You're more off your game than I've ever seen you. Come on. Wake up, for fuck's sake.'

'Beefhead? That's the first I've heard that. Is that a thing?' Paul says. 'I think I should have known about this before.'

'It's actually my own thing. I have to have something to think about that's my own thing when I'm checking and learning all this shite to teach you this shite and check your knowledge.'

'Beefhead,' Paul says and nods.

'Don't use it. Don't repeat it.'

'Well, it's in there now!' Paul says.

'Shite. Forget it. I've been reading *The Electric Kool-Aid Acid Test* and everyone's a "head" in there. Let's do the album quick-fire.'

'OK,' Paul says.

'*Strictly Personal*.'

'That's not the debut. *Safe as Milk*,' Paul says.

'I'm doing them out of chronology this time, amn't I? We haven't for a while but I'm just keeping you on your toes, amn't I, sonny boy? *Strictly Personal*?'

'A good sophomore. Ruined by the production. Phasing. Reverse. Too many fashionable hippie tricks,' says Paul.

'OK. *Unconditionally Guaranteed*?'

'Attempt at commercial breakthrough,' says Paul. 'An artistic failure. Um.'

'Tragic Band?'

'That's not an album...' Paul says. The sarge is looking at him and raises his eyebrows. 'Oh, right. The Magic Band... His Magic Band renamed Tragic Band by fans. Fans of Beefheart, that is. There's no fans of the album they did. Even Beefheart said don't buy it later on.'

'OK. *Doc at the Radar Station*?'

'Return to form,' Paul says.

'*Trout Mask Replica*?'

'We've done that.'

'Go over it again! I want tae hear it automatic. You know, like a gun.'

And Paul says, 'A masterpiece.'

'*Trout Mask Replica*?'

'A masterpiece.'

'Aye, good. *Lick My Decals Off, Baby*?'

'A worthy sequel to *Trout Mask Replica*.'

'OK. *Safe as Milk*? Quick!'

'Stunning debut,' Paul says. 'Stunned the record company because they had become more avant-garde between being signed and delivering the tapes.'

'OK. *Bluejeans and Moonbeams*?'

'Nadir. Tragic Band.'

'*Mirror Man*?'

'Do you know, I actually can get quite into that. The longer...'

'What?!'

'What? I'm saying it's one of the weird-sounding ones, but I quite like it…' says Paul.

'What? No Beefheart fan says they like or dislike the albums. Except the ones they dislike. You say something about the *time signatures* or *instrumentation*.'

'Beefheads?' Paul says.

'I told you to forget that. Now forget it.'

'It's just, on *Mirror Man*, first track, there's something like a harmonica solo, way out of tune, funniest thing I ever heard, I think. I used to sit through them and not listen, but last time I put it on—'

'Stop. Funny? Beefheart is *not* fucking funny. Jesus. No Beefheart fan *talks* like that.'

'Oh?'

'You losing this? Stick to the script. Counterculture. Beefheart. Musos. Free jazz and blues and that. Got it?'

'Sure.'

'Got it?'

'Sure,' Paul says.

'*Mirror Man* was released in nineteen seventy-one as the fifth album but was actually from an abandoned project from nineteen sixty-seven. Got it?'

'Sure.'

'And that's not a harmonica you're hearing on *Mirror Man*, it's a shehnai, given to Van Vliet by Ornette Coleman and played in a different key. Have you actually been reading the notes? *No one* plays out of tune. Got it? No one plays out of tune in Beefheart. Have you been staying vegetarian? I'll fucking kill you if you say you've been sneaking lamb shish kebabs again.'

'No,' Paul says. 'I mean, yes. Vegan, practically, now.'

'Good.'

'That's OK for you, is it?'

'It'll do.'

'Vegan,' Paul says. 'My guts are rotten.'

24

'Aye, right. Right, then. I've got to get off. I've got an evening of listening to grime lined up. If students get into it, well, we're fucked.'

1.14

The next time Paul is in Scotland Yard, four weeks later, he walks past an officer on the stairs with a box floating along at her décolletage, glimpsed between the lapels of a wool cardigan; then he notices a second in a corridor wearing the box with flashing lights – a pinhole pupil, is that? – sitting at the X of a kind of Zapataesque bullet belt arrangement across both shoulders. When he gets into the room with the sarge and the guv'nor, they're both wearing these same things, and the sarge is fiddling with his, stuck on the front of his stab.

'What's all this?'

'Body-worn video devices, sonny boy. We can record everything now,' says the sarge and goes for a pan shot by moving his torso from left to right. 'They've been trialling them. Hampshire or somewhere. They scare the fuck out of the scrotes, apparently. There's going to be a national roll-out, mark my words. I love it.'

'But—' says Paul.

'What do you think, guv'nor?' says the sarge.

'Aye, great. How have we lived?'

'But, hang on a second, here,' says Paul.

'What? What's bothering you?' the sarge says, and goes for a zoom-in by walking right up to Paul.

'Well,' says Paul, 'I mean, all mobiles have a camera on them now.'

'So?'

'So, if you start pointing those things at baddies, next thing is people will be putting their phones right up in your snout.'

'Aye? Naw,' the sarge says.

'Let the man speak,' says the guv'nor.

'This is the worst fucking idea since encouraging the Neighbourhood Watch Network. Jesus, the Neighbourhood Watch Network. Well, if finding out where the neo-Nazis in society are camped, then Neighbourhood Watch is the right way to go about it. Other than that, fucking rubbish. Fucking Stasi. And that was the worst fucking idea since PCSOs, fucking Mum and Dad's Army. No wonder they got us fucked on Forty-Four. Fucking hell, we need to wake up.'

'Naw. You think?' the sarge says.

'Yeah! Hi-vis vigilanties. But this camera thing. Shit, that's a bomb waiting to go off. It'll be like Neighbourhood Watchers form into militia with their own fucking cameras everywhere. That's when they'll realise half their problems are caused by… fuck-ups by the police and they'll go fucking feral.'

The sarge looks at Paul. 'Hmm. Mibby.'

'Maybe? Maybe? Any second now there's gonna be a whole lot of social media dedicated to showing shithead officers.'

'Christ,' says the guv'nor. 'They'll be finding out what absolute utter irredeemable cunts we all are. I mean, Charing Cross. Fuck. A carnival of cuntery.'

The sarge looks at the guv'nor. 'Hmm, the filth,' he says. 'Mibby.'

'It is going to be Mexican standoffs everywhere. Six cameras held up for hours on end used as acts of passive aggression. Yeah. We've already got us all inside cameraed-up fortresses. More gates, bigger gates, concrete blocks, more concrete blocks. Higher walls, higher fences, barbed wire, razor wire, palisade fencing and gates, mesh panels, chain link, bollards, rising bollards, falling bollards, spin guard, scaling barriers, raptor barriers, security spikes, sharktooths, barracudas, more concrete blocks, gabions. Anything we can think of, really. Cameras on everything.' Paul looks from the seated guv'nor to the standing sarge. The sarge looks at the guv'nor.

'Well, I like them,' the sarge says, apologetically, Paul thinks.

'And if all the cameras on walls are achieving anything at all, and it isn't achieving any more security for us, it's just saying we're behind our big walls and big gates and concrete blocks and we're scared shitless about all you scrotes outside them. *We* live in fear of *them*,' Paul says. 'We have nothing to be paranoid about but paranoia itself.'

'I see now. Shite. Fuck,' says the guv'nor, and he starts unbuckling or uncoupling or whatever the bullet belt arrangement.

'Naw. You think?'

'And now we'll be telling them we're scared shitless of them, crims, scrotes, Joe Public, everyone, when we're out and about.'

'Fuck. Fuckety fuck fuck fuck,' the guv'nor says. 'A total festival of fuckery.'

'You sure?' says the sarge, looking at his device.

Paul sighs.

'Right. Anyway, are you ready? Got something to say to the graduates?' the sarge says. Paul is looking at the body-worn. 'Look,' says the sarge, 'We can't fucking fix that now, can we? Are you ready, officer?'

'Yeah. Same as last time, eh? Tell them how we need intelligence, how we need intelligent intelligence, how we need intelligent intelligence gatherers. Blah blah blah. Mostly they just want to see a copper wearing jeans and a band t-shirt and Converse, think I'm fucking Serpico.'

'Hidden in plain sight, sonny boy.'

'Well, they're all too young these days to know what Serpico is. I don't know their equivalent.'

'*White Chicks*?'

'Come on.'

'*Kindergarten Cop*?'

'You're naming the comedy ones. I said *Serpico*.'

'*Reservoir Dogs*?'

'Oh, *Donnie Brasco*!'

'*21 Jump Street.*'

'OK, it's enough.'

'*Da Da-pah-ted.*'

'Naw, the original, *Internal Affairs.*'

'Enough!'

'Is this insubordination, constable?' says the guv'nor. 'You feel you can go shouting and bawling at your sarge and your guv'nor, constable?'

'No, guv'nor.'

'No. Sir. Constable.'

'No, sir.'

The guv'nor is eyeballing him, his face twisted into something that looks sinister, Mr Hyde to his Dr Jeckyll, then twisting further into a grin. 'Cunt,' he says.

'Thought you were proper angry there for a minute, guv,' says the sarge.

After Paul has delivered his piece about intelligently intelligent intelligence gathering (and, yes, he does pile these up to make this joke) he looks to the sarge, who steps forward and says to the graduate recruits, 'Right, so, that was great. We got any questions? You'll all want to know the tricks of the trade, no doubt, and Paul here, he's the Indian rope trick master.'

Silence.

'Anyone?'

'I'll go,' says one of the young women.

'Go for it,' Paul says.

'Well, we're just coming into the Met,' she says.

'Yeah, graduates, great,' Paul says.

'So, you've ended up in a kind of... specific area of policing?'

'Yeah, "specific" is one word for it.' He smiles.

'What got you into this area, do you think?' the young woman says.

'Wow. Great question,' Paul says. 'Give me a sec.' He looks at the sarge, just collecting his thoughts. 'OK. Maybe it's as simple as a pair of Clarks Commandos I had as a kid. You know, Wayfinders? No? None of you? None of you with parents, fathers, really, about my age? No?'

Blank faces.

'Well, there were these shoes which, in the heal of one shoe, had a little compass in it. Yeah! Cool, right? Maybe "cool" is uncool to say these days. And noting that "cool" is uncool. Anyway. You used it out and about, you know, knowing where north is, following a map, maybe.'

'I did orienteering... once,' says one of the Freshes.

'Yeah, that's the job! Orienteering, using a compass and map and getting yourself about. Good man,' Paul says. 'I always liked the feeling that, first, the compass was hidden, you know, in your shoe. And it was a useful piece of kit, something you could deploy, get you into and out of adventures. Maybe it was something as stupid as that. Always liked using a compass and a map, because it made me feel, when I could see the magnetic field on the earth, like a bird, along with a map so you could see more of the land, kind of like God or something, looking down on the world and seeing things we common mortals just can't see, like the old X-ray specs, you know? No? Nobody?'

'The punk band?' a Fresh says.

'Aye, we have a music fan in, eh?' says the sarge.

'The novelty item the band was named after, a pair of... well, you either get the idea or you don't,' Paul says. 'You people do know what a map is, right? You got how to use a compass and map in school?'

Some nodding, some shaking heads.

'Not all of you? Did you know about this, sarge?'

'Eh, aye,' says the sarge, 'from the kids, when they were learning to drive.'

'They don't know how to use a road atlas?'

'Naw, no really.'

'An A to Z?'

'Naw.'

'You don't know this?' Paul says to a random head shaker.

'Nope,' the Fresh says and smiles.

'How the hell do you get about, then?'

'TomTom.'

'TomTom? Oh, satnav!' Paul says. 'Totally? No maps as well?'

'TomTom only.'

'You trust those things, do you?'

'Yeah.'

'Sarge?'

'Aye, I've got a satnav. No TomTom, though. Do not know what it's called. Wife got it. No a TomTom – they're a bit old-fashioned now, hin't they?'

'Well, I've been using it since I started driving,' the Fresh says. 'So it's an old one.'

'Yeah, we just got ours when the kids were learning to drive, last couple of years. They said they wouldn't use the car unless we got one,' the sarge says.

'You don't read maps?' Paul says to the Freshes.

'Aye, well, you'll have to get it when the girls are ready,' says the sarge.

'Suppose I will. But relying on some big eye way up in the sky… I don't know about that. I don't trust it.'

One super-fresh-faced rosy-cheeked Fresh – looks about primary-school age – pipes up, 'What's it like to not be who you are? I mean, what's it like to be not who you are?' There's a ripple of laughter through the other Freshes. 'You know what I mean,' the questioner says.

'Yeah,' Paul says. 'Yeah, I know what you mean. Can I put it this way, turn it around, show you how normal this all can be? I'd say that you, you, you, or you, all of us, in fact, you're not who *you* are, not to other people. Well… I mean. Do any of you watch *The Wire*? Yeah? You? And you, OK. It's brilliant, intit? That ending, you know?'

'You mean the journalist bit?' says the sarge.

'Nah,' Paul says.

The sarge points an *I've got the idea* finger in the air. 'McNulty's redemption?'

'Nah,' says Paul, 'the way each of the characters' roles, gang boss, booster artist, et cetera, are replaced with younger versions of themselves, and you also know the ones we have been watching are just reiterations of previous versions of them, too. Anyway, my favourite episode is the one when McNulty has to go undercover as a British guy. Now, of course, McNulty is played by the English actor, eh, Dominic eh, what's the guy's name? West, yeah, West. So an English actor playing a Baltimore policeman pretending to be an English guy. I think people call that 'meta', don't they? Not sure I know about that, but you're graduates, so you'll know what that's all about. You lot eat books for breakfast.'

One Fresh, who looks nothing like a copper ever should look, pipes up, 'It's called involution in Nabokov.'

'Is that so?' Paul says. 'Involution?'

'Yes,' says the never-a-copper Fresh.

'Hang on. Nabokov? Sarge?' Paul says.

'*Lolita*,' says the sarge.

'Oh! That reprobate! Nobody should be writing books about teenage girls getting abused, should they? Or am I wrong?'

The sarge pushes his hands out, gesturing he has no idea.

'Anyway. *The Wire*. Of course, I think somehow it's inevitable that to stay in character McNulty has to make a pretty bad fist of doing an English accent, because he would, wouldn't he? So he does a sort of Dick Van Dyke 'cor blimey, dum diddle diddle aye' Lahndahn accent. So, but, really, that's an English actor, who has had some stick, apparently, for getting a part in American telly, like Idris Elba as well, and getting the accents right or wrong, if you see what I mean. So who is playing who? I mean, I think I've said that in a bit of a confused way. Anyway, back to what I was saying about you're not being who *you* are. Even the people who love you, your family, your friends. Forget it. In their heads you are their version of you. Look, look at it this way. I never liked the band Queen, right?' Another ripple of laughter. 'I know, I know, a copper who doesn't like Queen. Hardly adds up, does it? I always thought... the only thing I really liked about the band was John Deacon, you know, the bass player, 'Under Pressure' and 'One Vision' and the rock bit of 'Bohemian Rhapsody'. Some of his driving songs, driving the band along, you know? Deacon was like the real driver of their power, I thought. So anyway, Freddy Mercury dies, you know. 1991, it was. And then, I think after that, it all comes out, the lifestyle, the AIDS, the *coke*, you know.' A raised eyebrow from Paul, and more laughter. 'Well, Freddy. There was a reason they were called Queen, am I right? He was, like, king of the queens, you know? Naughty boy. So, I walk into the living room of the place I was sharing at the time with a couple of other lads, you know. Layabouts, the lot of us. This was when I was working sites before I saw the light. We were getting pissed every night and getting to know each other pretty well. They worked sites, too. Plastering, mostly, keeping the wolf from the door, though the way we were drinking, you know that dry fucking dust never got out from the back of your throat, that smell, and that feeling, no matter how many pints of lager you stuck down you, we were pretty close to the wolf pack a lot of the time. The lads, they're watching a Freddy Mercury tribute concert, I think it was Seal, you know, that singer with the scars, that, you know... forget it, you're too young, but you'll know the song, 'Who Wants to Live Forever', and this Seal bloke he's giving it his all, belting it out, total emotional crescendo. And I'm saying, "What's this all about?" and one of the lads says, "Freddy Mercury tribute gig, you know, for AIDS, AIDS benefit," and I says, "AIDS, eh?" but I'm thinking about John Deacon, what John Deacon ones will get played, so I says, "Have they played 'Another One Bites the

Dust'?" And both the lads turned to me and they, plasterers, remember, both of them are saying things like, "That's pretty low," and, "Ain't you got a heart?" And I was all, "What?! I like the Deacon loud-bass-playing ones." But in their heads I was the cu— shit who says AIDS deaths are just, you know, another one bites the dust, another flaming gay gets his. That wasn't me. But no matter what I said... See, I had to accept that they were going to think of me from then on as the guy who denied he was making derogatory remarks about gays and Freddy and dead young men, but they would also experience it *as* a denial. They thought and still think I am that person. I can't change it, no matter what I was thinking, what my truth was. And you'll never be able to change the you that is inside my head, just these fu— fleeting figures I've come in on now, maybe we'll get to know each other, but you get my point. You cannot change it. You cannot change it. Live with this. There is no you. No you projecting out into the world that holds your truth. Accept that and you are where you need to be with being a UC. Now you all think I'm a cu— shit. Fair enough. Doesn't change that this is the truth. Not any one person's truth. *The* truth.'

He looks around the fresh faces of the Freshes and knows he has got through to them. Time to polish it off.

'At one point during the summer when I was seventeen I became convinced my old mother was checking my pockets. So I started putting stuff in there for her to find. Cigarettes, a joint a friend gave me...' An 'OOH!' goes round the room. 'But, but, hold on, but which I never smoked, some white powders that were actually flour or icing sugar in little plastic bags, condoms, bits cut out of pornographic magazines, just to see what happened. I felt then, not now when I look back on it and regret playing such a game with her, but then, then I thought that the deal was sweet. I knew even if she found these things she couldn't bring it up because that would be to admit she was prying into *my* private business, which must be the greatest crime to commit against a seventeen-year-old boy. She never said anything if she did find these things, so there was no sweet pay-off, no win, nothing, not even vindication that I had caught her catching me out. Sometimes you won't know. That's when you just have to leave it.'

One of the other Freshes asks, 'Does it feel exciting to be undercover?'

'Oh, yeah, definitely!'

A ripple of laughter.

'No, actually, I'm not exactly sure what aspect you're thinking of…'

The Fresh gives it another go. 'Does it feel like you are in on something, how society operates and that, that most people wouldn't know? Just don't know?'

'Right,' says Paul. 'I get you. Let me think. Yeah, look at it this way. Last night there was one of them DEC appeals on the telly. You know, the Disaster Emergency thingy. Harrowing pictures. This little kiddy is covered in dust in a… you saw it? Yeah, awful, wasn't it? Little boy, I think it was, crying, covered in dust, in a wrecked, sort of bombed-out, I guess, building – you'd have to guess this was his home until kaboom, you know, and you could pretty much guess the family, the kiddy's mum and dad, maybe his brothers and sisters, all blown away. And then the little kid, he's wiping across his nose and because of the dust and his snot and tears mixing, the swipe goes jet black. Dunno why that detail got to me, but it did. Harrowing, just harrowing. Yeah. Anyway, what I'm saying about knowing what the hidden world is like, this hidden world that you think I get to peek into, and I guess I do. Yeah, I do. You're right, I do get to peek behind the scenes. Well, I'll tell you, the DEC put that little kid on the telly, break some hearts, get some money sent to some good places for a change because to put the more harrowing pictures on screen is filed under "Too hard to bother" – it would be the pictures of nice men and women in nice offices and government buildings, you know the sort of thing, computers on all the desks, nice, ergonomic chairs for H and S, had their full workstation assessments and everything, nice businessy suits, the main man in the glass-fronted office off to the left, you know the set up—'

'Sounds like *The Office*!' says a Fresh.

'Yeah, you're right!' says Paul. 'I am thinking of that programme, aren't I? And the places I'm talking about are that mundane and funny. Well, the point is that these are the places where the structural problems that lead to the little kiddy wiping his own tears and snot and dust into a black disgusting mess wiped across his cheek in the bombed-out home of his mostly dead family. Sorry, but that's what it's like looking behind the scenes; behind big bad scary Wizard of Oz is people doing spreadsheets.'

Paul looks at the sarge, who says to the Freshes, 'Well… thanks for that.'

Paul's walking from the room when the sarge is making more noises about hearing from an experienced officer from a very specialised field.

When the sarge gets back from his duties with the Freshes, he just stands for a moment with Paul, who's sitting on the table in their usual interview room next to the guv'nor sitting on the plastic chair, and clears his throat.

'I know,' says Paul. 'Tell me what you want me to tell them next time, then.'

'Did I say anything?' the sarge says.

'Don't have to. Shit.'

'Fuck it. We can all have off days.'

'I seem to be having more off than on at the moment.'

The guv'nor rises from his chair, gathers himself, straightening his tie and tucking himself in, then walks out of the room.

'Oh, eh, aye. Listen, eh…' The sarge takes out a piece of paper, hands it across to Paul.

'What's this?'

'Something you want,' the sarge says.

'Oh?' Paul looks down at the piece of paper. An address of a flat in Hackney.

'But I'm not giving it you because you want it.'

'No?'

'Naw. I'm giving it you because I think you might need it some time.'

'What is it, the Nosey?' Paul says, folding the paper in half, into quarters.

'First guess. Nice,' says the sarge. 'Still got a bit of a detective in there somewhere, hin't we?'

'I guess,' says Paul.

'Aye, right.'

1.15

[How do we look to the people in that plane? Julia wondered.]

1.16

Walking along in Hackney, he won't say what for, is when it comes to Paul where he'd seen her before, because he has seen her before. The blonde hair, the legs, even the red lipstick, even the way she flicked her hair and settled it behind her ear. She didn't look so young professional then, must have been a student, it was that kind of march. STOP THE WAR. TONY BLIAR. All that. And my God, she was a right little cutey, in spite of all the angry shouting and punching the air. That added to it, in fact. She was wearing this sort of dungarees thing, but with short trouser legs, hence the being able to see the knees and that, and recognising them in the pub. Then the weirdest thing imaginable happens. He sees her. Right there and then, as he is thinking about her, as though the sudden memory of her conjured her out of thin air as a magician's trick. Walking along past the traders at the Columbia Road market. He thought he could smell her perfume (and he gets it now, a memory of a former life, when he wore it, Paco Rabanne), and then, BAM, there she is. She turns up Ravenscroft Street and he feels a tingle as he stands at the corner and makes the decision to follow her, or his body of a policeman just naturally does this, he's not sure. A threat. An opportunity to find out more. It's rich with reasons as to why he should, so he does. You go towards danger, put yourself on the line, thin blue line, need to know.

She turns into a place on the Peabody Estate, he clocks the entry door and the CCTV entry system – it doesn't do to go into these details right here.

When he returns two days later at dusk, he does an explorat-ory ringing of the bell, standing off to the side of the camera. When there's no reply he goes to take up position. Then, just on a hunch, he walks down to outside a pub he just passed moments before. And, bingo, there she is, with a man and a woman who could be a couple and she's giving it all that with the hair flick and the settling her hair behind her ear. She's a looker, there's no mistaking. Well, we'll see about that, missy.

Around half-past ten she leaves her friends in the pub and walks back towards the Peabody Estate. Sorry. At 22.27 she leaves her friends and proceeds in a northerly direction, back towards the Peabody Estate. She doesn't look inebriated to any great extent. Hardly a 91 of the 1967. He imagines, for a second, putting his hand out to her, running up from back here, her hair swinging as she turns to meet his eye, no sound but a kind of 'ooof' ima-gined, his arm around her neck, the way her pretty legs move, a physical arrest, control and restraint. The thought has him hard and he thinks about where, between here and home, he could go for some privacy. Keep it discreet. Or he could visit his favourite lap-dancing club. He'll decide on the way home.

He returns again four nights later. The new studio he's working at with the label exists in the imagination a street or two away. Hipster Hackney. The other People's Republic. He checks her local as he passes first time, but there's no sign. As he passes on the other side of the Peabody, he stares at the window he feels sure is hers and there's a light on in it. He keeps it moving and walks up Shipton until he comes back on to the Columbia Road, crosses, and takes a seat on the low wall behind a green area and shrubbery of some sort, on the way into the old Guinness Trust Building. He plays with his phone for a moment, playing for time, lets his mind wander because he's not sure what to do about what he's doing right now, or why he's even doing it. The environmentalists who won't be happy until humanity is killed off and Nature can blossom in all its beauty, he's thinking. The vegans that do want every farmyard creature bolted, burned and buried. Slaughter isn't pretty but the rolling fields of the NATURAL world will be restored after all the stinking, shit-caked livestock are stunned and shunted to places of disposal. Environmentalists, he thinks, with shot-guns moving slowly through cities saying, 'You are the problem,' before BLAM, end of problem.

That's where she finds him. She's standing over him holding her coat closed and she says, 'What the fuck do you think you're doing?' Paul looks up from his phone and goes for a smile. 'I said, what the fuck do you think you're fucking doing here?' she says.

'Don't jump to conclusions,' Paul says.

'Don't jump to conclusions? OK. What conclusions do you reckon I'm jumping to?'

'Well, I don't know, but just hear me out.'

'This should be good.'

'I think it will be good for you. Just keep breathing and listen to me, can you?'

'Go on, then.'

'I've been asked... allowed to talk to you.'

'Yeah?'

'Breathe.'

'So why did you just come to... Why didn't you contact me the way I asked?'

'I never kept that, did I? That was binned as soon as I was out the door.'

'Well, you could have looked me up online.'

'I didn't get your name or anything. You kind of sprung everything on me.'

'So what are you doing hanging round here? That doesn't make any sense.'

'I was given certain pieces of information about you – they gave me information so I could track you down.'

'They? The Met?'

'I'll tell you all you need to know once we start talking. Now, do you fancy a drink or what?'

'But why didn't you just come to my door?'

'Dunno. Natural snooping, maybe. I case joints before diving in. Naturally cautious, just wanted to see the place first, then I came here to get into character before coming back.'

She's thinking about all this, playing a chess game in her head.

'How about that drink?'

She turns, looks around, turns to where she has just turned. 'There's one down there,' she says. 'One drink, right?'

'Yeah.'

'One.'

'I said yeah.'

Her perfume intensifies (and it's definitely like Paco Rabanne, but suitable for a woman, smelling good on her) as they sit across from each other, their drinks sitting, waiting, mostly ignored.

'Go on, then,' she says. 'Tell me some lies.'

'Come on, we can't start like that. Um. I don't know what to call you.'

'Natasha.* Tell you what. I will listen to you, right? But then I'll decide what to make of it, whether it's lies or not.'

'You don't miss a trick, do you? That's all the chance I'm asking for.'

'OK. Go on, then.'

'You getting anywhere with the story you want to do? Got a paper interested?'

'Working on it. We'll see where it goes, shall we?'

'I guess we all work like that a lot of the time – see where things go.'

'I guess we all do.'

'So, I'll just come out with it, shall I?'

She waits.

'OK. They want me to talk to you. They even gave me your address to make contact.'

'Anything in writing to prove that?'

'Nah. Come on. Just like you, they gave me a scrappy piece of paper. I had to memorise it and eat the piece of paper.'

She raises an eyebrow.

'OK, I didn't eat the paper. I ripped it up and binned it.'

'And why do they want you to talk to me?'

'I don't know. They move in mysterious ways. The exchange of information between the… public and the media and the police is a tricky business. Like a chess game.'

'Do you play chess?'

'In this context I do, yeah. Or maybe it's that I'm one of the pawns. Does it matter either way?'

'And I get to be another pawn?'

'Do you think we get to be anything else? That would be, no offence, naïve.'

'Maybe. What if all I want to do is watch the game, do the sports report?'

'Calling chess a sport?'

'Could be considered that way.'

'So they want you talking to me.'

'Who's "they"?'

'You know.'

'Do I?'

'I won't be coy. The Met. It suits their purposes for the time being.'

'OK. OK. Interesting.'

'Yeah?'

'Mmm.'

A sip of wine.

'And you can see it's not lies?'

'I didn't say that.'

'But it will get you what you want?'

'Yes. Maybe that *is* the way I have to look at it.'

'Always measure by outcomes.'

'Mmm.'

'Look, forget the rhyme and reason, or what they're looking to get out of it. Do you want to set up something so we can talk?'

'We're talking now.'

'Not for much longer. In a public place? Not the best idea.'

'Can I get confirmation from… "they" that they are allowing this?'

'Encouraging it.'

'Yes. Do you think that would be something I could get?'

'In a word? No. They are a wee bit more cautious than that. You get to talk to me, but that's it. If you're really interested in the whats and whyfores I think they want the story to get out there in a… controlled way. Pre-empt some outright lies with some of the truth.'

'The *truth*!' And she laughs. 'And you're OK with all this, are you?'

'Nope. But I'm not sure I have… I told you, I'm a pawn. I know I'm a pawn.'

'So. What's in this for you?'

'Holding on to whatever protection they can provide for me, helping them protect me, my… wife and kids.'

'OK. I can see this is difficult for you.'

Paul shrugs. 'Pawn,' he says. 'However…'

'"However"! That sounds interesting.'

'Well, it's just…'

'Yes? Come on.'

'Well,' Paul says, 'it's just there's some people saying that there's some money going around.'

'Do they now?'

'Yeah, they do.'

'I've heard that, too.'

'Any confirmation on that?'

'I'd need to talk to "they", wouldn't I? Not your "they", my "they". You know what I mean?'

'I do. Tell you what. This is about done.' He lifts his pint and drinks it down. 'But I think I should talk some more to my "they", and you should talk to your "they", and then we go from there.'

'Sounds agreeable as far as it goes.'

'Yeah.'

'Yes. How will I be able to contact you?'

'Same way as you got me last time.'

'Well, to be honest, that was a bit of a trick I'm not sure I could swing again.'

'Well, I suppose I've got more tricks up my sleeve than you, so I'll be in touch with you.'

'Doesn't necessarily sound fair,' she says.

Paul stands, shrugs, leaves.

The planes for and from Heathrow, for and from Gatwick, for and from Stansted, criss-crossing the sky ominously, always ominously now, don't the buildings seem to reach up to them or don't the planes seem too low, too low, too near, hanging like unexploded missiles in the sky, ever since that September?

But then a bus can blow up under you, beside you, on to you. Welcome to the paranoid world. J.G. should have written one about Borehamwood called that. She's in her flat, taking the Olympus out of her pocket with hands that are still a little shaky from the thrill of it, maybe the fear of it, too.

1.17

Paul doesn't feel able to head home, not after that. He makes a phone call and heads to a pub near his home in Islington. He needs his mind taken off. When he arrives, Patrick* is already there. Patrick is the only person he keeps in touch with who actually knows who he is (not strictly in a professional capacity). It's a bit dangerous keeping the friendship going, especially so close to home, but Patrick and Paul go way back, did their training together, can rely on each other, can drop whatever fucker they are supposed to be to the world in front of each other. Patrick is undercover, but drugs squad, so he's not so mental as Paul is, Paul thinks.

'Awlriiiight?' Patrick says.

'Yeah,' says Paul. 'Everything OK?'

'Well, country's going to the dogs, yeah?'

'Yeah, I know.'

'You know what it is, with the country going to the dogs, dontcha?'

Paul starts laughing. 'Go on, then,' he says.

'It's the bloody Blacks, innit,' Patrick says.

'Yeah,' says Paul. 'Fucking Blacks.'

'Yeah, bloody Blacks. Going to the dogs, mate.'

'The Blacks, yeah.'

'Mr and Mrs Black, yeah?'

'Yeah, Mr and Mrs bloody Black, the old couple, yeah?'

'Yeah, the Blacks at number... number...'

'Thirty-eight?'

'Yeah, the bloody Blacks at number thirty-eight, bloody…
white supremacists.'

'It's not right.'

'Fucking Nazis, the pair of them!'

'Fascists!'

'Bloody racists coming round 'ere.'

'Ruined the country, mate.'

'Yeah!'

'Yeah! Fucking Mrs and Mr Black the bloody racists, fucking
white supremacists, coming round here—'

'To number thirty-eight—'

'Coming round here with their bloody ideology of racial
purity and superiority. Fuck me!'

'It ain't right!'

'No.'

'Nahoh.'

'Nahahahoooo.'

The two of them collapse into giggles, can't believe how
fucking funny their old joke is.

'Do you want a wee…' Patrick says, raising an eyebrow and
tapping his nose.

'Nah, those days are behind me. I told you, since the girls,'
Paul says.

'Lightweight,' Patrick says, and heads to the toilets; is in
there for about ten minutes, comes back out sniffing, holding
alternate nostrils closed then looking around and pulling his
zip up.

'Right, fuck that,' Paul says.

'Fucking hell,' Patrick says, 'I did finally give it a go. Are you
joking? And you have to listen to it all the fucking time? Aw, mate.
Trout Mask fucking *Replica*? I mean, what the fuck is going *on*?'

'I know, right? Though the weird thing is, after a while it's
normal music that starts sounding weird when you've been deep
down inside Beefheart.'

44

'Fucking hell, mate. My heart started bumping funny during parts of it, I kid you not.'

'Yeah, I know.'

'What you've put me through!'

'Yeah.'

'Tell me again how they got to that for you?'

'Aw, they were looking for a way to set up my deadkid ID, and they said, what's the craziest music you were ever into? And I said, well, I used to listen to John Peel, seventy-eight, seventy-nineish. They were like, excellent, who did you like? And I said, one song won't go away, 'At Home He's a Tourist' by Gang of Four, you know. So the sarge goes off and investigates that, and he comes back to me with, well, Gang of Four is good, but they don't exist any more – let's think of something still going. Next thing he's back at me saying, you like John Peel, eh? And I'm, yeah, you know, did, not now though. And then the sarge asks me if I hadn't heard one of Peel's perennials, Captain Beefheart? I said I didn't think so. He says you must have heard Beefheart. Peel still playing it and all that. I said maybe I just didn't notice. I mean, it was really just the ih ih' (Paul makes a gesture of very aggressive air guitar) 'of post punk. I mean, I didn't even really like punk.'

'Every copper loves the Pistols, though,' Patrick says, supping lager. 'And The Clash till they went funny. Why didn't they let you just stick with Morrissey?'

'Because they'd have wanted it to be The Smiths, because that was hippy-punk-lefty Morrissey, wasn't it? I'm not spending my time listening to that whiney shit.'

Patrick says, 'Yeah. As soon as he'd left the band he was straight away better, more direct, funnier.'

'Exactly,' says Paul. 'Wait. I haven't ever known the music you're supposed to like in your life.'

'Because we don't do it that way in our MIT. We can like the music we like.'

'What? I never knew that. Doesn't sound, you know, professional.'

'Fuck you.'

'Anyway. The Smiths? Not all that boohoo-me whingeing about this and that and pity me.'

'Fucking Marr, wasn't it? Wet fucking blanket.'

'Yeah, Marr. Nominal determination, that. He marred everything.'

'Stephen turned his sights on the world and the world was a cesspit. Even things like his vegetarianism. It's a kind of hard man, I've got this right, you've got this wrong straight-edge thing. Bloody minded. And, of course, he loves the furries. And the music. Just compare something as weak as my first shit like 'There Is a Light that Never Goes Out' with something as muscle-flexingly discordant as the start of the *Viva Hate* album, 'Alsatian Cousin' or something.'

'Yeah. And he's starting to get good images together, something more coherent. 'Suedehead' and all that. Even the most Smithsy song, 'Everyday Is like Sunday' has a better swagger. But he's still not quite there yet.'

'Let me check my phone. Yeah. Of course 'Margaret on a Guillotine' is just hilarious, but it's all still a bit navel-gazey. 'Kill Uncle' doesn't do much, but 'The Harsh Truth of the Camera Eye'? Off kilter.'

'But then *Your Arsenal* kicks off psychopunk and fuck, the thing's back on. Next up, a stomp, next up, some mad noises, next up, infamously, 'The National Front Disco'. By now he really knows what he's doing.'

Now they're both checking their phones, scrolling through Wikipedia on the Morrissey page.

'Yeah, he can do anything, sound like Marc Bolan, laugh his way through a song, Pink Floyd it, German shit. *Vauxhall and I* and he can do epic. Fuck me.'

'And the jokes are even funnier, not like the faux fey shit of The Smiths years. Not so poker-up-the-arse. *Southpaw Grammar*? Kicks off on an eleven-minute Morrissey song? Fuck me sideways. Mad. Drum solos, screaming, 'Dagenham Dave', fucking malice, then another ten minute mini-Brechtian opera to finish off.'

'A *what*?'

'Sarge has been educating me again. Things get even more crazed on *Maladjusted*. The quiff's gone but the anger rises to new heights. All ammunition. But then there's a spoken-word thing.'

'Yeah, *Maladjusted*'s not one of his best.'

'Almost like the early artsy-fartsy stuff with the band. When we get to *You Are the Quarry* he sounds a bit confused, don't you think? But still not as fuzzy-headed as back in the day.'

'And the takedowns and piss-takes are spot on. The fuck-off of 'Irish Blood, English Heart'. Fucking angry. All good. The super-fuck-off of 'I Have Forgiven Jesus', ultra-fuck-off of 'I'm Not Sorry'. Straight down the fucking throat.'

'*And* an album cover with Morrissey toting a machine gun!'

'And 'All the Lazy Dykes'. What's that about? *Ringleader of the Tormentors* starts off with probably the full lift-off of Morrissey's musical career, finally. He's confident enough to sing a piano ballad, chucking in instruments, voices, noises, what could almost be a Status Quo song, and is that a gong on there!?'

'Yeah, the lyrical adventurousness, the melodic complexity, yet guitars that seem to hark back to those punky Sex Pistolly days tipping full tilt into an orchestral piece. It doesn't get better.'

'Except it does, with *Years of Refusal* where he goes full Johnny Rotten on the first track, thank you, drop dead. Then it's a gallop through some of his best and most glorious noises, Krautrock noises, flamencoish noises, getting almost Mexican with Morricone whistles and horns, the bent saw as musical instrument, feedback, space noises, strings, more horns, radio noises.'

'All sorts.'

'What will come next, do you reckon?'

'Well, for someone getting better with every step, only greater and greater things have to lie ahead. He really is our Bowie, keeping moving, clarifying, making his argument for himself ever more forcefully.'

'Brilliant.'

'Good things will come.'

'Yeah.'

'Have to.'

'Yeah.'

'He's been kind of quiet lately.'

'Yeah.'

When the chat turns to Paul's annoyance at the Met not giving him some information about himself, they're being clammy bastards, Patrick says, 'What you want is an SAR under the FOIA.' Then they both start laughing really hard. 'Yeah, that'll work!' Paul says.

They end the night laughing as they make for the toilet together.

1.18

People involved gather in Trafalgar Square from as early as six in the morning. They – they being our family – arrive at a quarter past eight, alongside about half the contingent of ORGAN:EYES, with the aim of meeting with the other half at the fourth plinth. The march will kick off around ten, moving as slowly as possible, for maximum effect on traffic in central London, heading down Whitehall, past Downing Street, into Parliament Square past the Houses of Parliament, then along by the river to Tate Britain, just like last time. Sophie, at least, is in high spirits. It's only the second time Liv has wanted to be on one of the big marches and it's Sophie's first big one. They have been on countless smaller marches, stood in streets behind trestle tables, at fundraisers, and been on one sit-in (they got to stay awake all night while Paul dozed in and out of consciousness from about three in the morning onwards and their mother spoke to students about this revolutionary this and that environmental that the whole night, and the girls were frazzled when the morning came, sleeping most of Sunday and still tired and sleepy when Sunday evening came). The sounds of whistles is prevalent. As they wait by the plinth more and more ORGAN:EYES people show up, admiring Sophie's hand-painted sign. From the south side of Trafalgar Square people are starting to move towards the top of Whitehall. The crowd reconfigures to allow more to join from where the National Café is and coming along past the Sainsbury's Wing of the National Gallery (Prince Charles's famous 'Carbuncle', Julia is explaining to Sophie, a story she has never heard before). It's like a funnel emptying, the way the crowd begins to move, looking from the top of Nelson's Column, or from the helicopter that buzzes and circles overhead. In their part of the crowd the shouts start going up, 'THE EYES OF THE WORLD ARE ON YOU!' and 'OUR EYES ARE WATCHING!' A chant that sounds mechanical and low-pitched, 'WE WATCH, WE SEE, WE WATCH, WE SEE, WE WATCH, WE SEE, WE WATCH, WE SEE, WE WATCH, WE SEE,' rumbles from just ahead of them as they begin to move away from the fourth plinth. 'Who's that?' Sophie asks. Her mother looks at the statue she's pointing at and replies, 'I'm not sure, but that's Nelson,' pointing to the column in the middle of the square. 'Who's Nelson?' Sophie asks. 'Remind me to help you look him up when we get back,' Julia says, 'but he was an imperialist pirate is all you need to know for now.' 'Boo!' Sophie says, laughing. Liv sighs and carries her placard horizontal in her right hand, not up where it can be seen. When they reach the funnel down in Whitehall they see the size of the police presence and it's much more than Paul expected.

Involuntarily he says, 'Jesus, what the fuck?' He looks over to Julia and nods. 'Full riot gear, no waiting, except for shields,' he says. Julia checks the girls are just ahead of them. 'Feels different,' she says to Paul. 'They're just feeling grinchy because of the last one. Couple of incidents. They hate it when the tactics change in the crowd, but they're going to have to get used to it. MySpace and Facebook is fucking with them a way email and texting just can't. People can actually see what's happening streets away. They're probably shitting themselves,' Paul says. 'There're kids here,' Julia says, looking back at him as she swings up close to the girls just ahead of Paul. 'It won't come to anything – the fucks just want to be tooled,' he says. But as they pass close to the police line he can see that although there was no evidence of shields from further back, they are on the ground by the officers' feet, held up at an angle and rising to their knees. Julia is looking from them to the girls to Paul. 'It'll be OK,' he says. He looks around. 'Stick together.' Then he catches up and gathers Julia, Sophie and Liv to him as best he can. 'Where are we meeting if we get split up?' he says. 'We know,' Liv says wearily. 'I want to hear everyone repeat it,' Paul says. 'Back at the fourth plinth,' Julia says, followed by Sophie repeating exactly these words. Then Paul raises his eyebrows looking at Liv, saying a few seconds later, 'Liv?' 'Fourth plinth,' she says. Paul and Julia look at each other, and Julia gets her mobile phone out to start taking pictures and filming short snatches of film of the crowd, the helicopter above and the police line. Along into Whitehall Paul, Julia and Sophie start to add their voices to the people around them in their part of the crowd. Mostly 'THE EYES OF THE WORLD ARE ON YOU!' and 'OUR EYES ARE WATCHING!' directed at the police line, but when Paul starts a very enthusiastic call of 'You say TORIES!' Sophie is so happy to be able to join him in swearing, as she believes it to be, 'We say SCUM!' 'You say TORIES!' 'We say SCUM!' 'TORIES!' 'SCUM!' 'TORIES!' 'SCUM!' 'You say TORIES!' 'We say SCUM!' Paul laughs as his younger daughter bounces and skips and raises her whole body to shout, 'WE SAY SCUM!' Then Sophie begins her own call of 'WHOSE STREETS?' and a good number of the young people around her hear her high but loud voice and answer 'OUR STREETS!' 'WHOSE STREETS?' she calls, like she is genuinely and insistently asking whose streets these are and a wave of young voices, added to with more adult voices respond, 'OUR STREETS!!' Then for a while the calls and responses go on around them and Sophie is saying to Liv 'Who is that?' of a statue as they pass. 'I have no idea,' Liv replies, coldly, then she puts her arm around Sophie's shoulder and smiles and calls out 'WHOSE STREETS?' And Sophie is overjoyed to respond, 'OUR STREETS!' and Liv goes on doing this for a few minutes, bouncing along with Sophie as they do so. Voices mentioning Prince Andrew, the Duke of York, ripple through the crowd towards them. Julia moves closer to Paul and says, 'What are they all on about Andrew for?' 'I suppose it'll be about that Sarah Ferguson story, in the *News of the Screws*. Half a mill for business contacts or something, last year, I mean this year... last year,' Paul says. 'She's in debt up to the eyeballs.' They listen as they walk along to more people saying something about Prince Andrew and Sarah Ferguson, but they can't quite make out what's being said. As the crowd moves forward towards Downing Street the number of cameras, still and video, increases, mostly mobile phones amongst the crowd but also pros, journalists, at the edges of the crowd, either static or walking alongside, and then a good number of EG officers. As they get to Downing Street Julia falls behind Paul and watches as he looks towards Scotland Yard when everyone else is directing their eyes and voices towards the gates of Downing Street. When he looks back he says, 'Crime solving doesn't happen. We all know the numbers for burglary convictions, rape. The only thing that keeps us safe is that most people are concerned, law-abiding citizens, getting on with it, or the ones that are so fucking stupid that they infer a million laws and rules around them that aren't there. Society by consent and policing that just runs around being police, doing police-like stuff. Blues and twos, they love it. Forty-fouring all over the place. But that's it. You know the fastest growing crime? Fraud. You know what they're doing about that? Not much. Forty rozzers in twenty cars with blues going, blasting out of a station at fifty does nothing about that.' 'Yeah,' Julia says, 'The Prick.' 'What's that?' Paul says. 'Just something I heard. The Prick. Private Dick. You know, a play on a private eye.' 'HUH?' Paul shouts as the crowd gets loud again. 'Just, a private eye, Private Eye, Private Dick.' 'CRESSIDA?' Paul shouts. 'Yeah,' Julia says. In their contingent Paul joins in as the shouts grow louder. 'WE ARE WATCHING! THE WORLD IS WATCH-ING! WE ARE WATCHING! THE WORLD IS WATCHING! WE ARE WATCHING! THE WORLD IS WATCHING!' and again the rumble of 'WE WATCH, WE SEE, WE WATCH, WE SEE, WE WATCH, WE SEE, WE WATCH, WE SEE, WE WATCH, WE SEE.' Now there are a number of people looking at Scotland Yard, where there's a thick police line, maybe three deep, and the shout goes up and is joined, 'PUBLIC SERVANTS! SHAME ON YOU! PUBLIC SERVANTS! SHAME ON YOU!' and 'WHOSE POLICE? OUR POLICE!' One woman, really pretty angry, Paul thinks, is shouting into the face of one officer, 'WE PAY YOUR WAGES, MATE! WHAT DID YOU DO AT WORK TODAY, DADDY? SHAME ON YOU!' The crowd slows to almost a standstill as they reach Downing Street and the call and response returns to 'You say TORIES!' 'We say SCUM!', with both Sophie and Liv almost screaming 'WE SAY SCUM!' After a few minutes the mass of people begins moving slowly forward, then about forty or fifty people seem to move to south of the crowd and begin doubling back up Whitehall, again with the names of Prince Andrew and Sarah Ferguson being men-tioned, and then the shout from one of the stewards, 'Come on, Prince Andrew!' Many of them are checking their phones for text and Facebook and MySpace messages and emails. Paul checks his phone, but can't see anything – certainly nothing about Prince Andrew. There's a lull in the voices around him and also, because people are doubling back, a space in the crowd he can move into next to one of this Prince Andrew contingent. They're singing the 'Solidarity Forever' song, but because they're moving in the other direction the song dies on the wind. 'Mate,' Paul says, 'what's all this about Prince Andrew? Did he die or something?' The voices around them rise again with a 'WHOSE STREETS? OUR STREETS!' and Paul has to move close to the Prince Andrew guy to hear his response, but it's fragmented in the din of voices and whistles, which are being joined by an almighty racket of plastic horns. 'NAH, MATE,' Paul catches. 'ANDY AND SARAH. THE STRAND. IN TRAFFIC. CAUGHT. 'KIN SURROUNDED, MATE. WASTES OF SPACE!' Paul nods and heads back to his place beside Julia, who gives Paul an *I'm curious* look, shouting being probably beside the point now. But Paul gives it a go and they hunch their shoulders together and he directs his voice into her ear: 'I think Prince Andrew and Sarah Ferguson are caught in traffic up on the Strand and people have got them surrounded. Some protection officers are going to get their arses served to them on a plate for this. Jesus. Who are they?' 'Anarchists,' Julia says, 'nutters.' 'Jesus,' Paul repeats. As they come closer to Parliament Square a man with a microphone in his hand comes up alongside Sophie. When she stops calling out 'OUR STREETS!' in response to 'WHOSE STREETS?', 'Are you OK to talk?' he says breathlessly. 'It's for local radio.' 'Sure,' says Sophie, 'what?' The local radio man then looks at Paul and Julia briefly, as though waiting for them to stop him, but there's only a pause and then he says, 'There's lots of kids here today, like you.' 'WHAT?' Sophie shouts into the microphone being held out to her. The local radio man jumps a little and rearranges his earphones so they are beside his ears rather than on them. 'I SAID, THERE ARE A LOT OF KIDS here today.' (The sound of the crowd dies down as it does suddenly every so often.) 'YEAH!' Sophie says. The local radio guy lifts his mic to his own mouth and says, 'Do you think it's right that so many kids are here, doing this?' 'YEAH!' Sophie says, 'WHY NOT?' 'Well,' the guy says, 'do you understand all the things people are protesting about here today?' 'WHAT!?' Sophie says, maybe mishearing, maybe indignant. 'Do you understand all the things people are protesting about here today?' he repeats. 'I understand what I'm protesting about!' Sophie shouts and Liv starts to laugh and says, 'YAY! Sopheeee!' 'AND WHAT'S THAT?' the local radio man says. 'DIDN'T YOU HEAR ME?' Sophie says, 'THESE ARE OUR STREETS, WE CAN PROTEST ALL WE LIKE!' 'Is that so?' local radio guy says. 'Maybe it's you who doesn't understand what's going on?' Sophie says. 'Well, now…' local radio says. 'But you're just little kids. I mean, who cares?' 'WE DO! WE CARE!' Sophie, utterly defiant, says. Julia is smiling, but she can feel tears welling up in her eyes and her vision mists. She looks over at Paul and he looks in the same state, like the pride in his daughter might just burst out through his chest *Alien*-style, in the most unpretty way possible, SPLAT. Police and stewards seem to be trying to direct people away from the Houses of Parliament and up Great George Street, around the other side of Parliament Square, but it's a fairly half-arsed operation and more and more people are either on the grass or walking along in front of Parliament. A smoke bomb goes off and Liv shouts, 'LOOK!' and she's pointing at the Winston Churchill statue, which has acquired a bright green grass Mohican. Smoke is rising sideways above Parliament Square. Paul joins them laughing at the effect of the huge bronze statue topped with bright green. Then Sophie is asking Liv who another statue is and Liv says, 'Disraeli. An old prime minister.' Julia feels proud again, now for her other daughter, her knowing this. 'Was he a Tory?' Sophie says. 'Think so,' says Liv. 'Scum?' Sophie says, and Liv shrugs. As they turn a corner back to face the Houses of Parliament, the contingent around them start chanting, 'SCRUTINEYES PARLIAMENT! SCRUTINEYES PARLIAMENT! SCRUTINEYES PARLIAMENT!' 'I'm not sure that really works when it's said out loud!' Paul says to Liv and she replies, 'Mmm.' Then she starts shouting, 'SCRUTIN EYES PARLIA MENT! SCRUTIN EYES PARLIA MENT!' making the ORGAN:EYES gesture with her fingers which says that she is watching, in this case, Parliament. Liv nudges Sophie and both of them laugh and do the gesture as they chant. As they pass the MI5 building the crowd go quiet, almost silent, then quietly and en masse people start saying, 'Shh', 'Shh', 'Shh', then it grows loud as more quiet voices join together until it sounds like, 'SSHHH SSHHH SSHHH!' and the sounds overlaps until it sounds like a weird ocean. At Millbank Tower some people try to occupy the reception area. 'Anarchists?' Paul says to Julia and she shrugs. Territorials arrive and a shout goes up, 'MUSCLE! Muscle, everyone! MUSCLE!' But, once the doorway is cleared, the Territorials don't seem to feel there's much to do and they stand down fairly quickly. They seem to disappear round the side of the building somehow. Paul is saying, 'Something does feel different this time,' when there seems to be a haemorrhage of black amongst the colourful clothes of the crowd and a single shout goes up. 'KETTLING! KETTLING! They're coming to kettle!' Paul and Julia turn to each other like it's the end of *Bonnie and Clyde* and move to quickly stand either side of Liv and Sophie. They try to move faster, further ahead, trying to get to in front of Tate Britain, where, for the moment, there seems more space between people and fewer officers. 'What's kilting?' Sophie says, as Paul and Julia hold a hand at the back of Liv and Sophie respectively, their other arms forming a kind of waving opening and closing boat bow, hoping that people will move aside for them, which, when they see the girls, most people do. But it's hopeless – the police line is moving too quickly, whipping round in a well-rehearsed spiral that tightens at speed, to shouts of 'PEACEFUL PROTEST! PEACEFUL PROTEST!

PEACEFUL PROTEST!' 'They'll keep us here for a wee while,' Paul tells Soph. 'Don't worry, then they'll let us go in little dribs and drabs.' 'This is terrible!' Soph says, and she looks more angry than worried. Suddenly there are officers cutting them off from getting closer to the Tate and for a moment they backtrack, so that when the police circle forms then thickens they are close to the centre of the crowd that has been surrounded. As the circle tightens the people inside move closer and closer together. There are horns and whistles and voices shouting and back behind them the approaching sound of militaresque drumming, but where they are starts to feel like the calm eye of the storm. Another kettling circle is forming with stragglers from the first circle. Some people within the circle at the circumference start scream-ing and shouting not words but just throaty, rasping vowels. Paul looks at Soph and sees fear on his ten-year-old daughter's face; she's on tiptoe trying to see what's going on, holding on to his shoulder. He doesn't mean to, so close to her, but he says, 'FUCK,' and looks around himself, at Liv, at Julia. But then minutes have passed, twenty, twenty-five, with none of them speaking. The circle stops contracting and becomes static as the kettling reaches half an hour, forty minutes. Paul's looking at his watch, checking the time on it against his phone, he's not sure why. 'Are we going to be here for hours?' Liv says. 'Mmm, maybe,' Julia says, then looks at Paul with a look on her face he can't quite read. 'It looks like a developing tactic,' Paul says. 'They want us to want the exit,' Julia says. 'Hold us longer, get rid of us quicker.' Another few minutes and there is a piercing scream at the police line and again Paul and Julia look at Sophie and then at each other. Julia pushes her back against the two people behind her, then another two, then moving round to face the police line, then another two, as she uses her arms and legs and facing forward motion of her whole body, angled into the crowd, who are becoming individual objects she has to move aside and between till she gets to the police line. Liv and Paul and Sophie, as best she can, follow Julia's movements with their eyes. After a few more minutes they see her arm waving from a place to the left of where she was, beckoning them. Paul takes the hands of his daughters for the first time, it feels like to him, since each was a toddler or small kid, and they work themselves into a triangular formation, spearing their way forward to Julia. When they get up to her she nods to one officer in particular and the police line just open-sesames for them. They and a few others trickle out of the cell. 'I told them Sophie has seizures,' she says to Paul, and he gestures something like *you have to do what you have to do,* Julia thinks. It's been about an hour in all. But before they get far, suddenly batons are here, there and everywhere. Shouts of 'PEACEFUL PROTEST! PEACEFUL PROTEST!' rise all around them. Officers are pulling at a woman in a wheelchair. She's screaming, 'BISCUIT! BISCUIT! HEDGEHOG!' Someone else is shouting, 'IT'S JESS! SHE HAS TOURETTES!' When she grabs desperately at the arm of her own chair a baton comes down on her knuckles. 'BISCUIT! HEDGEHOG! BISCUIT!' she shouts. Paul steps forward, pulling at a police officer, shouting, 'WHAT THE FUCK ARE YOU DOING? WHAT ARE YOU DOING, OFFICER? OFFICER! OFFICER! CONSTABLE!' Still, he has the presence of mind to notice the television news reporter and cameraman pushing and shoving to set up so as to capture this, and he turns and runs, disappears from sight into the crowd. Trick you have to learn. Christ! The cameraman had a PRESS bulletproof on him like he's in fucking Afghanistan. Maybe just back from Iraq, because that's more or less over. For us, anyway. Shouts of 'Peaceful protest! Peaceful protest!' recede as Paul drags Julia, Liv and Soph fully out from the kettling, past a crowd of protesters surrounding a small group of mostly women police officers, holding their mobile phones up to film them and shouting, 'WHO'S KETTLING WHO? WE'RE KETTLING YOU!' and, confusingly for Paul, 'YOUR JOB'S NEXT! YOUR JOB'S NEXT! YOUR JOB'S NEXT!... YOUR JOB'S NEXT! YOUR JOB'S

NEXT! YOUR JOB'S NEH-EXT!' and, confusingly for Julia, 'NICK CLEGG, SHAME ON YOU! SHAME ON YOU FOR TURNING BLUE! YOU'RE ONLY YELLOW TORIES, YOU'RE ONLY YELLOW TORIES, NAH NAH NAH NAH, NAH NAH NAH NAH!', and she looks around trying to see whether, somehow, on the off chance, Nick Clegg or another recognisable member of the Liberal Democrats are in this mêlée, noting her brain's use of this word, and with accent and circumflex in place. Both of them are confused when the shout dying out around them is 'Miss England, you are my darling!', and neither of them are confused when one of the last things they hear clearly is 'Mayor Johnson, go fuck yourself!' Julia, being pulled by Paul, pulls at Liv who pulls at Sophie and they all move forward to the very margins of the crowd in front of Tate Britain, where gallery security are manning one door, letting people who want to see what's going on exit the building past rudimentary graffiti on the wall, a slapdash semi-cursive spray-painted 'tory scum' next to an erection, then the word 'REVOLT!' The family break formation and drop their arms as they approach the half-closed, half-open door that the security are half-heartedly manning, but when they approach, having straightened themselves into the resemblance of tourists, visitors, family-day-outers, there's some surprise as they stroll in past the security and people exiting. In the quiet cool of the building they turn to each other and stifle laughter. It feels like a full escapology trick, from out there, in all that noise and shoving, to this freedom of movement within an almost empty, almost silent (except for the now muffled sounds of the noise outside) gallery. 'Come on,' says Paul, gathering himself. 'We can go see Douglas's piece that's in here.' 'Uncle Douglas has a work in here?' Liv says. 'Yeah,' says Julia, 'It's not all in Tate Modern.' When they track the right room down, Douglas MacDougal's *TWENTY-EIGHT DAYS* is on a plinth sitting across from Tracey Emin's *CV: Cunt Vernacular*, and the girls start to giggle hysterically, totally getting the vapours at the name of Emin's video.

They'll see in the news tonight that some kettling circles last for nine hours, with Chief Inspector Jane Connors defending the kettling. No footage of the assault on the disabled woman is shown, even though they watch all bulletins on the channel the reporter and cameraman were from.

2.17

Two days later Paul gets an anonymous text to call another number, one he doesn't seem to recognise; his brow furrows, staring at the number for a long time. When he calls the number on his other phone he says, 'It's Paul Dorian.'

'There is a problem after all.'

'But I thought you said—' Paul says.

'Am I going to have to repeat myself just now? Right now? Right now, when time might be tight?'

'No,' Paul says.

'You always knew... Look, pal, I know it's not what you want.'

'No,' Paul says. 'Just tell me what it is.'

'Breakdown.'

'Right.'

'OK?'

'Has to be, doesn't it?'

'Aye, we have to stage a breakdown. Get your actor brain switched on. Get into character. OK?'

'Yeah.'

'Going to have to do it with the simple motivation. You know the one. The one where the distraught actor says to the director, "I just don't know who this character is; what's my motivation?" And the exasperated director, he's like, "Your motivation is to cross from upstage left to downstage right. Now just do the fucking scene." You remember?'

'Yeah.'

'No other thinking about the character.'

'I've got it.'

'You're going to go to a GP. I'll tell you in a minute. It'll cover your tracks, bit of credibility. Everything will be fine. Little time out, lay low. Everything is fine. We'll review after that.'

'How long?' Paul says.

'A few weeks. A month, maybe.'

There's a pause.

'Right,' Paul says.

'Right?'

'Yeah.'

'Look, call me back on this number in ten minutes – I'll give you the rest of the information then, right?'

Paul listens as the call-ended tone sounds, stares at the phone in his hand, then up and around himself. A walk to a public telephone, repeating the number in his head to memorise it. Then he drops the other phone to the ground, looks around himself, sees no one about, stamps on the phone twice and puts the pieces in a litter bin before walking past two public phones to a third. We see him at this phone, phoning the number he has memorised. 'It's me. OK. OK. Yeah, I can write this down.' He can't write it down, hasn't anything to do this with. 'Where? And what's the name? What is that, a code name? Just seems a bit unusual. Kafka. Proctor Kafka? Oh, Doctor Kafka. That's definitely fake, whatever it is. Because. Kafka? Spell it. Oh, right. Cath Carr. Right, missus – yeah I'm writing it down – Cath C. A. R. R. Yeah, got it. Contact details?' Paul closes his eyes, concentrating, memorising. 'OK. Yeah. OK. Yeah. OK. When?' He looks at his watch. 'What, I can't go back to the— Right. OK. Yeah. Yeah, I bet you do. Yeah. Right.' He walks away from the phone, orientates himself towards Harley Street and starts walking.

He waits in the waiting room for an hour, then goes in to see Dr Kerr – her name's on her door. Not Carr: Kerr. Not a GP either: a psychiatrist.

After a moment, 'How are we today... Paul?' she says.

'OK,' Paul says.

'And how can I help?'

'I thought you had the details.'

'Details?'

'Yeah. You know what's happening, right? I kind of assumed you knew what was happening.'

'Happening? Lots of things are happening.'

'Yeah, but, what's happening between us.'

'I received a referral, if that's what you mean.'

'From the police?'

'From your own doctor. Why would the police be involved?'

'My own doctor? Doctor Linehan?'

She checks her notes. 'A Doctor Fabius.'

'Right. Right. I thought you were in on it.'

'In on *it*? In on what, Paul?'

'Why I'm here.'

'Why do *you* feel you're here?'

'Um. Breakdown. A diagnosis, I suppose.'

'Well, let's not rush into anything, shall we?'

'I seem to have all the time in the world on my hands now.'

'What makes you think that?'

'Listen, are you going to write me up for something and then I… I don't know, head for my parents' house or something?'

'Is that what you want to do?'

'I thought it would go something like that, yeah.'

'Are you running away from something… Can I just check something? Do you feel safe?'

'Safe?'

'Yes, safe.'

'Well, there are a lot of factors in anyone feeling safe, aren't there? What aspect of safe do you mean?'

'Just… safe.'

'Um. No, not particularly safe. Wait, are you using "safe" in some specific way? Some psychiatric way?'

'Yes, I am.'

'So what does it mean, "safe", in the way you mean?'

'Safe. Safe from danger. Safe in that something terrible isn't happening or about to happen.'

'Well, I think some terrible things are about to happen to me, yeah. I mean, my whole world just went…' and he makes a gesture and noise with his mouth.

'Your whole world?'

'Yeah. Look, can I check your referral notes to get a better understanding of—'

'What do you feel you don't understand?'

'I just need information to understand, to be able to help you.'

'You feel you're here to help me?'

'No. Yes. I mean… Help each other, eh? And if I just knew—'

'I think we should talk for a while longer before we come to any conclusions. Have you been taking any substances, Paul?'

'What? No.'

She moves to make a note. 'So you deny any substance abuse.'

'I don't *deny* it like I'm refusing anything. I'm just saying I haven't been taking any drugs. I drink a little. In moderation. What are you getting at?'

'I'm not getting at anything. Feel reassured, it's just ways we have of saying things. Like "safe". It's just a way we have of saying things. So you "deny" substance abuse and you "deny" feeling suicidal, I think you are saying?'

'Woah. Where did that come from?'

'Oh. So you don't deny feeling suicidal?'

'I said I don't *deny* anything. This is taking a weird turn.'

'So you don't deny feeling suicidal?'

'I… hang on.'

'Take your time.'

'I'm starting to feel confused. Are you going to write me up for some diagnosis? Should I contact the Met, or try to get through to Fabius?'

'Is there some medication you should be on?'

'What?'

'The Met? Do you mean the police? What would we need them for?'

'To clear this mess up a bit.'

'You feel the police can help you with your confusion?'

'Yeah. Look, I'll come clean. I'm in the Met.'

'I don't really mind where you work. I'm not sure it's pertinent to our discussion today.'

'I thought it would be pertinent as pertinent goes. Look, can I just have a look at the paperwork you've got there?'

'Let's talk a little while longer first.'

'I don't think there's anything to say until you let me see the paperwork.'

'Let's talk. We're just talking.'

'No. I want to see the paperwork. This is confusing. I need to see the paperwork.'

'We're just talking.'

'Are you going to let me see the paperwork?'

'We're just talking.'

'Give me the paperwork.'

The heavy mob arrive, three of them, two of them hands on, white coats and everything.

She must have an alarm under the desk or something, or maybe this is all on camera. She writes him up for a Section 2; 72 hours for assessment. This paperwork she does give to him.

2.16

The hospital sits in grounds that under other circumstances you might call pleasant. A rich, thick lawn and something that you could call woodland at the end of the long drive. When he arrives at the double door of the bungalow building of red brick, he's shown into a faceless reception room, sits on one of the four chairs.

A nurse joins him and straight off Paul says, 'I think I'm here due to an… administrative error. I'm kind of faking this.'

'Oh? You are?' the nurse helping him says.

'No,' Paul says, 'I mean really.'

'We know,' the nurse says. 'It's OK,' he says, 'we get a lot of it.'

'It's like in those books,' Paul says, 'Um, Heller's *Catch-22* or the other one, um, you know, um, Ken Kesey's *One Flew Over the Cuckoo's Nest*. You seen that film? I'm just following those examples and making out like I'm nuts.'

'OK,' says this nurse. 'We'll work with you on that.'

Paul says, 'Work with me on that? What do you mean?'

The nurse says, 'We can work through all the things you're thinking – it's no problem. It's the job, really. What we do every day.'

'But are you listening to what I'm saying? I'm saying I'm fooling you. I just need some time out of my real life,' Paul says.

The nurse nods and says, 'Real life. Right.'

'Are you sure you can hear what I'm saying?' Paul says.

'Yes, well,' he says, 'we get a lot of it. Honestly, you are unique, but your experience is not. Trust me, we're professionals.'

'But,' Paul says, but then he just mentions the books again.

'It's OK, everything is OK,' the nurse says. 'You're in admissions and evaluation now. Everything must feel a bit up in the air for you. Shall we get you settled in? I'm going to go through your bag now. Is that OK? We just have to… you know… sharps and things like that.'

Paul waits as the nurse searches through the backpack, then he says, 'You people are mad.'

'Oh?' the nurse says. 'We're mad?'

'I'm telling you I'm feigning this,' Paul says. 'I just need to lay low because of this sort of… conspiracy I'm part of.'

The nurse says, 'Oh? Conspiracy?'

Paul repeats, 'You people are mad.'

'It's enough of a typical experience in your position,' the nurse says. He smiles, nicely.

'My position?' Paul says.

'Look,' he says, 'whatever you're thinking, I think you need some help to work it through. It's part of your journey.'

'Do you think the conspiracy I'm part of...' Paul starts, but then he stops talking and looks at the perimeter wall he can see out of the window.

'I think maybe you should get some sleep,' the nurse says. 'Relax. You're in a safe place.'

'Safe?' Paul says. 'Yeah, that's what I'm looking for.'

'Well,' the nurse says, 'you've found it. You are safe now.'

'Yeah, safe,' Paul says.

2.15

After two weeks of this supposedly 72-hour assessment, Paul is chatting informally with one of the nurses when the nurse says to him, 'Is it OK, as we're talking, that I have a look at your notes? Just so I can get to know you both ways, and so I'm sure of what you're actually telling me.'

'Sure,' Paul says. 'It's OK. I don't mind.'

'It's just, you know, things can get...'

'Sure,' Paul repeats. 'It's OK. I don't mind.'

'It's just, you know, I heard you were part of this Satanic conspiracy—'

'*Satanic*? I didn't say Satanic. I said state. *State* conspiracy.'

'See, just exactly things like that,' says the nurse.

When she returns with his folder, they sit side by side in the ward garden talking some more and the nurse is saying, 'Oh', 'Is that right?', 'And what about now?' and other comments like

this, keeping the dialogue rolling. The nurse follows on after colleagues when they come past trailing a tiny young woman who is
screaming. Paul looks blankly at the page of notes that the nurse
has just turned to and on it he reads, 'Paul believes he is part
of a "nationwide conspiracy" – involves him having been living
under an "alias", identity gained (somehow) from dead baby,
ect. He is an "undercover police" working for the "deep state".
The "conspiracy" involves police officers apparently marrying
counterculture figures who they (have to?) have children with –
thus "infiltrate and destroy [this] counterculture." He has been
"undercover" for more than twenty or thirty years! This delusion obviously bears some markers of recent newspaper reports
ect of concerns about undercover policing in the newspapers,
and Paul himself has mentioned the CO INTEL PRO in the
United States (check this) but contains a number of grotesque
details (such as the dead baby, the deep state ect) – these added
in and reflect irrationality of the delusional framework. NB
Common conspiracy theories about "deep state" ect.' Paul
twitches on the picnic bench. He rolls and lights a cigarette and
stares off to the wall that encloses the garden for a long time
until the nurse returns. She closes the file over and says, 'Oops. I
probably shouldn't have left that with you. Still, it's all stuff you
know yourself. You could do a subject access request to get eyes
on it all, anyway. Paul?' He stares at the wall. 'Paul?' she repeats,
moving her head closer to his. 'Paul? Is our conversation over?
I thought we were getting along quite well there. Paul?'

Finally, Paul says, 'Yeah, well, you know… *Trout Mask Replica.*'

'Sorry? Paul?'

'*Trout Mask Replica*. The Mascara Snake. Fast and bulbous,
you know?'

'Is there a reason you're thinking of these words?'

'Well, Harkleroad, Zoot Horn Rollo. Very prevalent in the
mix. *Mirror Man*, the shehnai,' Paul says, then he starts making a
noise as best he can like the shehnai on *Mirror Man*.

'Paul, I don't think we can get anywhere if you're not going to try and make yourself—'

'*Doc at the Radar Station*. Return to form.'

'Come on, Paul, we were doing so well there.'

'*Trout Mask* masterpiece. *Lick My Decals Off, Baby*.'

'Paul—'

'*Safe as Milk*.'

Later, Paul hears the nurse at the nurse station talking to a colleague. 'And then he just… stops making sense, a whole jumble of words that are just meaningless. It didn't seem aggressive or anything, but…'

'Don't worry. It happens. And it's not aimed at you. He's communicating with everyone that way now,' the other nurse says.

This for about a week until, during a team consult, with a couple of faces he's not seen before, a senior psychiatrist brightens and smiles and checks the notes in his lap just as Paul has started responding. And the senior psychiatrist says, 'So, you're a Beefheart fan, too? Cool.'

2.14

Into weeks four and five Paul reduces his communication to one repeated phrase, with slight variations. 'I want to die.' 'Of course, I want to die.' 'Oh, how I want to die.' 'You know, don't you, that I want to die?' He tries to keep track of the variations so that they are as incongruous as possible. His notes say, when he next catches sight of them, 'NoT responding To TreaTmenT. In facT, sTill deTerioraTing.'

'It's interesting,' he says.

'It's interesting?' the nurse says, the one who first talked to him and settled him in. The nurse looks at the most recent note himself and says, 'It's interesting that you're not responding to treatment?'

'Nah,' Paul says. 'The way the person writes all Ts upper case.'

The nurse says, 'Hey, you're talking to me.'

'I guess, yeah,' Paul says.

'Yes?'

'I think it's time to move on, now, yeah.'

'So the "I want to die" phase is over?'

'Yeah,' says Paul, 'sorry about all that. But still nothing's working. They've changed my mix of antidepressants for the third time in four weeks. Handbrake turns. No titration.'

'Something will feel different soon,' the nurse says. 'What are you on now?'

'Californian rocket fuel. One of the old lags was telling me it sends mentalists psychotic and sane people barmy.'

'You don't listen to them, do you?'

'What? Those nutters?'

Paul and the nurse smile. Paul starts rolling his fifteenth smoke of the morning.

'And how are you feeling on that combination?'

'I won't lie to you, I'm feeling a wee bit twirly. Like I'm always floating.'

'Are you laying off the benzos? I saw you asked for one yesterday.'

'I'm still jumpy.'

Paul sits for most of the next ten hours in the day room doing next to nothing. The next morning, after meds and breakfast, Paul goes into the television room and sits in front of reruns of *Frasier* on Channel 4. 'Hilarious, this, innit?' he says to the other patient in the room, who is fumbling around in a cupboard.

'What?' the other patient says, looking up and around from the interior of the cupboard.

'*Frasier*,' Paul says, pointing at the television. 'I mean, it's about a psychiatrist. Who's more crazy or wacky or whatever than the people he talks to about their problems.'

'What?'

'I mean, it's about a psychiatrist… and we're in a mental hospital.'

'What do you mean?'

He gives it another go: 'It's the episode where something goes wrong for Frasier.'

'Oh yeah?'

'Yeah,' Paul says, 'but by the end Frasier reaches a deeper understanding about his relationships, to his family and to the world at large…'

'Oh, that one.'

'Forget it,' Paul says. 'Forget about it. Forget that I said anything…' He turns back to watch *Frasier*. 'Anything at all… anything…' As it approaches the second episode, Paul stands up and walks through to his room. He goes into his wardrobe, pulls out a knotted pair of socks and stares down at four pills of Zopiclone he extracts from the knot. Then he stares at his bed, then the pills again. He sighs and puts the pills back in his knotted socks and returns to watch the end of the second episode of *Frasier*.

After this, Paul stares at the clock in the television room, rather than the television, until lunchtime. Patients enter and leave the room, usually after sitting and watching the television for only a few moments. After lunch, a patient who Paul has gotten to know a little, knows her latest and previous diagnoses, what medication she is on, what her opinions of the psychiatrists and ward managers are, what she thinks of Paul's medication combination now and of Quetiapine, which he had been taking until it seemed like he was developing psychosis, offers to make him a cup of tea. When they sit together sipping tea in the television room, both staring at the television still tuned to Channel 4, the other patient says to him, 'You seem a wee bit out of it today. Do you think the new ones are working?'

'Yeah, I'm fine,' Paul says. 'Just having difficulty sleeping whenever they think Zopiclone isn't a good idea. I can't get through a night then. To be honest, I've managed to keep a few aside, Zopiclones, but I'm trying to keep them for when I really need them.'

'I think we all do that with little favourites,' the other patient says.

'Yeah,' Paul says. 'Thing is, I think about taking one after breakfast almost every morning.'

'It happens. But they'll get really pissed off at you if they find out they're not tracking all your intake. They like to be in charge. If you get caught they'll put you back on obs.'

'I know. So what, really? I been on and off obs the whole time I been in here. Doesn't make much of a diff. They're watching us all the time, anyway.'

'Your speech is a bit slurry.'

'Yeah?' Paul says. 'I do feel… bit weird. I have this thing. I keep hearing these words going round and round in my head. You know, like, "Moon, Ella, liquorice, bulbous, Guru, bobbinet, Dachau, moonlight, dandelion. Atomiser. Floozy. Tapered. Blimp." And then it starts round again.'

'God. What is that crap you're saying?'

'Words. From *Trout Mask Replica*. The Captain Beefheart album.'

'Never heard of it.'

'No. Why would y'ave?'

'Are you ok?'

'Just, if that'd stop, then I'd feel better.'

'Do you think it is the new drugs you're on?'

'Listen, I'm just glad the doses are massive, and that they're letting me have benzos and Zopiclone again as well,' Paul says. When he wakes and opens his eyes, the other patient has disappeared from her chair. Paul turns back to watching what's on screen. An advert comes on for the store where every item is a pound in price. Paul watches and listens as the crashing discord of Beefheart's *Trout Mask Replica* opener

'Frownland' starts and then looks increasingly puzzled as the advert continues, the lyrics of the song altered to

You'll be happy
When you come to Poundland!

Our shops with full shelves and wide aisles
And a whole world of
Bargains and buy one get one free!
Those other shops
You won't return to soon
You want Poundland!
Walk on over to us
Come by car, bike or bus
Come down to Poundland!
Where you can queue with everyone
And everyone is buying
You're happy, not crying
Everything's a pound here
Seven items or less, we mean fewer!
Express tills for mums and dads and girls and boys
You all love us!

You'll be happy
When you come to Poundland!

When it ends, Paul gets up unsteadily in a dazed-like condition and walks through to the nurse station. 'Can you come and watch this, please? I'm not sure what's going on,' he says.

One of the nurses follows him through to the television room and sits and watches two rounds of adverts, but then says she has to go and do other things. 'Come tell me if it happens again, if you see – hear – what you think you hear again.'

She leaves and at the next round of adverts, the Poundland Beefheart one runs again.

Paul is mumbling, 'It can't. It can't be right. Can it? It can't be. I mean… um…' But he sits mumbling only to himself and wiping some dribble off his chin and doesn't go looking for a nurse again.

2.13

Absolutely, positively, the funniest, the most hilarious aspect of suicidal depressive episodes is the suicidally depressive mind's search for the weaponisation of everyday objects. This shower mount, that doorknob, this fourth-storey window. Everything around the suicidally depressive mind is a potential killer or potential killing machine. Yes, this electrical appliance, this bath, this extension cord; this kitchen knife; this rope in the attic, this car the suicidally depressive mind's body is behind the steering wheel of. Can the suicidally depressive mind encourage, cajole, somehow *make* the festering, stinking, decaying, dying lump of meat that surrounds it jump, from high up, or into this water? But there's no fun in these. This electric socket, though, can the suicidally depressive mind somehow plug this stupid body in? the suicidally depressive mind is thinking. Ha! How? By getting the flex for this lamp bare at the end and in one hand this wire and in the other hand this. What, so that the AC can throw you back and away and leave you half frazzled, but, crucially, alive? The suicidally depressive mind turns on itself. You fucking idiot, the flex would be better employed around your neck and tightened on… what? What? Oh, forget it! Is there nothing? Nothing the suicidally depressive mind can come up with? Half the suicidally depressive mind starts to stand back from the other half of the suicidally depressive mind, sneering, jeering, 'For fuck's sake, you, the other half of my suicidally depressive mind or you, this stupid, decaying, festering, stinking body, cannot do *anything* right. If you tried to throw the body off somewhere high up you'd only break your fucking legs, left alive *and* humiliated. 'Wait,' Paul says. 'What is it I'm thinking?'

But it's one time that really makes him laugh, laugh till he is in tears, laugh till he cannot breathe. He's being accompanied to the local supermarket by a bank nurse, his first time off the ward in days; weeks, maybe. On the walk down to the shop the bank nurse says to him, 'So, do you have a bedsit or something, somewhere in the town?'

'What?' says Paul. 'No. I have a house. Not here. In London. I live there with my wife and two girls. A bedsit? No. I'm not...' Worth the completion of that thought?

'Oh?' the nurse says, looking around himself, not looking as though he has heard what Paul has said.

'It's not like...' Paul says.

'Mmm,' the bank nurse says.

When he gets to the supermarket Paul realises he has not thought through what he might actually buy, now that he's here. The bank nurse, name unshared and unknown, starts to get restless, as though he has been fooled into something. What other purpose can a supermarket have, after all, if not to *buy* something? Paul picks up a Mars bar. Holding it, looking at it, he's thinking how he doesn't like Mars bars, but he doesn't want to enjoy the bar of chocolate he actually does like until... hm, what? He's out of here? Not *here* here, but out of the wards? Somewhere else? Back to whoever he once was? Something like that.

Sitting back in the walled garden of the ward with the Mars bar by himself, smoking and waiting to open the Mars bar, he suddenly materialises. I am here, he thinks. This wall, this grass, the sky. Everything materialises. Everything and him. He is here in this place, smoking, with a Mars bar.

If he were to tear open the wrapper, and get his thumb against one end of the Mars bar, and lodge it in his throat, pushing down, down, maybe into his windpipe, with his thumb which is there, there, his thumb which is there, then would this materialisation here, here, and here, stop? This is when he starts laughing. Laughing until he cannot breathe.

Late in the afternoon, when his dread is finally beginning to subside, Paul starts chatting to a nurse, built like a brick shithouse, about why he hasn't seen him, this brick shithouse, before.

'I'm redeployed today,' the nurse says.

'Re… deployed?' Paul says.

'Yeah, I usually work in the locked ward. Well, look at me.'

'Hm, yeah, maybe I should have guessed.'

'Gentle giant, me, though. I take it easy.'

'I've a guv'nor says that all the time, "take it easy".'

'Oh, *you're* the copper who's in here hiding? Right. Right.'

'Am I famous or something?' Paul says.

'Nope. Just I know what you're on about.'

'Is that so?'

'Yep. I know. I'll be honest with you, mate… What is it…?'

'Paul.'

'I'll be honest with you, Paul. I was in the coppers, good few years. Undercover, some. Drugs squad. Bit of gangs, vice.'

'You're… you're kidding me?'

'Nope.'

'And you know what I'm doing here? Why I'm in here?'

'Yep. It's an out, am I right?'

'You know?'

'Yep. This one seems to be going a little far, though. Are you sure you aren't mental as well?'

'Are you supposed to use terms like that?'

'What, "mental"? I'm from the locked ward, mate. We're a bit more… robust up there.'

Paul sits thinking for a moment.

'What you thinking?' Brick Shithouse finally asks.

'I was thinking, even though you know about why I'm here and all that, that won't do me any good, will it?'

'Wouldn't expect so. Like I say, maybe you are mental as well.'

'Like you say, yeah.'

'And I don't have any pull, not down here. Anyway, don't you think you're better off just taking it?'

'Taking it?'

'The time, the drugs, whatever.'

'I'll be honest with you. I think the drugs are starting to affect me.'

'They're supposed to.'

'Yeah, but affect me in a bad way.'

'What do you want me to say? That can be by accident or design. Sometimes we need people… calm, placid, you know? Receptive.'

'I don't feel placid, mate, I feel jumpy as Christ knows what.'

'Look, I'll give your case a gander, OK? See if I can make heads or tails.'

Paul sighs. 'You're probably right.'

'About waiting it out?'

Paul nods.

'Yep. They'll come for you when the time comes.'

'Yeah,' Paul says. Then, 'I didn't catch your name.'

'Call me John.'[†]

'Call you that?'

'Yep. John.'

Paul does not see John again. Paul does not see the debrief between Call Me John and his superior.

'Did that yield anything?' the superior says.

'Not much. I don't think it was really that great a strategy, to be honest.'

'No?'

'Nope. I'm not exactly sure what we were going for.'

'Well, you might be right. Where does it leave us, do you think?'

'He seems a little bit more reconciled to sit it out, take what's his.'

'Is he any clearer on the whole conspiracy delusion thing?'

'I think he knows why he comes across mental.'

'Do you think he's doing it all on purpose?'

'Oh, sure, yep. Man like him?'

'But is he… impaired?'

'Of course. Man like him? In here? Of course.'

'Of course,' the superior says. 'Right, back to the locked ward for you. Just one last thing.'

'Yep?'

'Were you ever really in the police?'

'Yep.'

2.12

When it's his turn to see Hamza and the team at the weekly review he, Paul, says straight off, without being invited to say anything, 'The drugs are driving me barmy.'

'Yes,' says Hamza. 'Have you considered that your illness is what is causing you to be, in your term, barmy, and that the drugs are in fact stopping you from being even more, again, your term, barmy?'

'It's just. It's just I was thinking suicidal thoughts. Sorry, I mean, having thoughts about suicide. Yesterday. About how funny it is. I mean. I mean. What do I mean?' Paul says.

'Yes, what?' says Hamza, staring at Paul, not letting his, as in Hamza's, gaze drop. 'You already went for quite a while saying you wanted to die. I'm correct?' He, Hamza, looks at a nurse, who nods.

'That was different,' Paul says.

'How so? Do you mean that you were saying it then but it is only now that you are thinking it, about suicide?' Hamza says. He, that is to say Hamza, pauses, though not quite long enough to allow Paul to both think *and* speak. Then he, which we have established is Hamza, says, 'Might I even go further to suggest that perhaps the drugs are making you increasingly less – your term – barmy?'

'Um, yeah,' Paul says. 'Because I wasn't barmy when I came in here.'

'Oh, that's right,' says Hamza. 'You say you are in here because you are a secret agent hiding from the—'

'Police officer,' Paul says. 'Undercover police officer, I admit, but just a police officer.'

'OK,' Hamza says, 'some sort of a spy, anyway.'

'Just police officer.'

'OK. And you were not ill, mentally ill, until we started to, what, feed you all these drugs?'

'Yeah, about that,' Paul says, 'how come the admission could be set up for me by the Met but when I get here for some sort of reason of authenticity I have to get the drugs down my neck?'

'Hmm?' Hamza says distractedly. 'Oh, we want you to get better.'

'But you are in on it, right?'

'In on it?'

'You let the Met get me admitted.'

'I'm not in on anything. Can you hear yourself, Paul? You see conspiracies that do not exist. You are mentally ill. We are here to—'

'Oh, now I get it,' Paul says, scanning the people in the room. 'Of course. Of course. Naïve of me. How could you lot be trusted? Of course you'd have to think this was all real. Me being a nut, not the conspiracy. You really think I am a conspiracy paranoiac. Ha! I can actually hear myself, doc. Funny.'

'So you understand the drugs are to help you, to make you feel better?' he, Hamza, says dismissively.

'Doesn't feel like that to me,' Paul says. 'It feels like they are making me increasingly barmy. Fucking barmy as a barn door.'

Hamza looks up from his notes sharply. 'This term I do not know,' he, Hamza, says.

'Don't worry, it's not you, I've never heard it before either,' Special Mike says to Hamza, then turns to him, Paul, and says, 'Is it regional, Paul?'

'No, I've never heard of it either,' Paul says.

'How do you mean?' Special Mike says.

'It just popped into my head. Rhymes. I don't know.'

'Barmy as a barn door,' Hamza says. 'Could be something. I've heard something like it.'

Most of the rest of the meeting sounds like a detuned radio to Paul. Probably sounds like a detuned radio to Hamza too, Paul thinks. But then he, Paul, comes to and he, Paul, is saying something about how things cannot really go on like this much more, by which Paul means for Paul, Hamza thinks, and that he, Paul, would be unable to be like this in front of other people and that he, Paul, could not see this happening. Jesus, Paul thinks, my thoughts are all over the place.

'Other people?' Hamza says. 'You have two daughters, is that right?'

'I have… um?' Paul has no recollection whatsoever of divulging real circumstances of his real false life, but he, Paul, must have, because Hamza can't just be guessing, can he? Weakly he, Paul, that is, says, 'Yes. Two daughters.'

'Say you go home and you feel like this, this inability to be like this, as you call it, in front of your daughters.'

'OK,' Paul says.

'Say, further to this you, being unable to be like this, as you have put it to me, you do something to escape either this feeling or your daughters.' Again the pause that allows Paul only to start thinking but not finish thinking and start and then finish speaking. 'Say, further to this, you commit suicide in the family home, in front of your two daughters,' he, Hamza, says.

Jesus, Paul thinks, what is Hamza driving? What is he, he being Hamza. Why this? What good can this? Paul is thinking these things, these incomplete things. His only complete thought is that he is thinking incomplete things. He is also looking out of the. Tears and his hands shaking. Looking. Finally he can look back at.

And Hamza shrugs.

Paul feels like a bomb. In other circumstances he would have said his mind was exploding, but that isn't the case here. No such catharsis is available. He, Paul, is a bomb, unending explosive potential, waiting.

And, he thinks, he being Paul, it's maybe because he needs her to that Julia materialises. He sees her back and her arm, moving out of sight, around a corner in the corridor. He can barely walk at more than a crawl, but he does what he can to speed up and catch up to her. Around the corner he sees her back. She, Julia, is walking away from him, not hurried, at a normal pace. Normal. But he's moving through space slowly; his legs won't lift. 'Julia,' he says. Quieter than he expected. 'Julia,' he says again – Paul that is – Paul says again. There are flashes at the back of his eyes, bright flashes of white and red and pink light, at the back of Paul's eyes, and in the white flash he loses sight of Julia, but just for a second, and she materialises in front of him, facing him, talking to him. She's wearing her pyjamas and a pair of socks and her slippers and she has a dressing gown wrapped around her, which makes no sense at all, Paul is thinking. And what is she saying?

'You needed me to be here?' she says.

'I... yes,' Paul says.

'Well, I can understand that,' Julia says.

'Yeah? Yeah,' Paul says. 'Listen, Julia, there's something I've got to tell you.'

'Go on, then, caller,' she, Julia, says. 'I'm listening.'

'I… I think,' Paul says.

'Yes?'

'I think I am actually becoming increasingly unwell in here.'

'It's a hospital. Not much use if you aren't unwell.'

'Yeah, but, listen. Listen. I think I was not unwell when I came in here. I was faking it.'

'You're sure?'

He shakes his head, trying to clear his mind. 'Fairly sure. I mean. It was all about something I can't go into right now.'

'Oh?'

'Yeah. Sorry. But listen. Listen.'

'I am listening. I'm listening.'

'Yeah, I know you are. But listen, what… what… I'm saying is I think the drugs, this place, the whole thing, it's making me worse, I think.'

'You think?'

'Yeah.'

'You might be right.'

'Yeah?'

'Well, you're hallucinating me right now, aren't you?'

'Yeah, I guess so. The pyjamas and that.'

'Spot on.'

'But I needed you.'

'I think this is something to do with projection.'

'Yeah. I think I heard that word before, from one of the nurses or doctors here.'

'That's probably why I said it just now.'

'Yeah. Yeah. Probably.'

'That would be part of projecting a hallucination, wouldn't it? Me saying things you've heard from people in here.' She looks off to the side. She's signalling the conversation is coming to an end. 'Yeah, well, that's a normal signal of that, isn't it?' she, Julia, his wife, says.

'I don't think I said anything there, though,' he, the man that is Paul, that is called Paul, says. Thomson or Dorian or something.

'I know. Doesn't really make sense, does it? Like the way you keep having this memory from recent days, but it's really a memory from the toilet block at your primary school,' Julia says.

'Yeah. Yeah,' Paul says.

'Do you think maybe you're asleep, Paul?' Julia says.

'Maybe,' Paul says. 'Certainly my mind playing tricks on me.'

'I wouldn't worry about it,' Julia says.

'No? No,' says Paul. 'Julia?'

'Yes, Paul?'

'It's just… I've got something to say to you.'

'That's OK. You can tell me.'

'It's just… It's just I have something important to tell you.'

'Go ahead. I'm listening to you, Paul.'

'Listen, it's just I have something… something I really have to tell you.'

'You can tell me, Paul. It's OK. I'll listen.'

'Yeah. Thanks. It's just I have this thing to tell you.'

The next day a new admission arrives from somewhere, trailed by a male doctor and three male nurse heavies. The new admission is by any measure agitated. He walks erratically to and fro, here and there, talking though not talking *about* much. 'So this is this' sort of stuff, 'and that's that, huh?' The doctor trails closest, talking quietly to him. He's tall, well built, the new admission man. The doc says, trying to orientate the guy, 'I'm a doctor. You're on a ward. You've been admitted. We'd like you to think about taking your medication. Is that something we can talk about?'

EVERY TRICK IN THE BOOK

'Something we can talk about,' the guy says flatly. 'This is a hospital, then, is it?'

'You've got it, yes, a hospital.'

The guy moves suddenly off to the left, and the heavies rearrange their configuration. There's a weird thing to being mental, Paul is thinking, you look as though you have superhuman strength.

'Can we talk about your medication?'

'My medication? Am I on medication?'

'Well, we don't think you've been taking it. That might be a problem. We'd like you to think about taking your medication.'

The guy looks sceptical.

'Can we at least talk about that?' the doc says.

'Sure. What medication are you on?'

'I'm pretty sure you don't need to know if I'm on any medication. I'm the doctor.'

More sceptical staring, and the guy rocks forward and back on his heals. 'Mmm,' he says. 'Give me a minute.'

'Take all the time you want. Can I repeat some stuff?'

'Mmm.'

'I'm a doctor. These are nurses. We want to help you. You're on a mental health ward of a mental-health hospital. Do you remember? The police brought you in a while—'

'The *police*?'

'OK. We don't have to dwell on that bit just now.'

'The police. Yeah. I'm in the police.'

'Are you sure?'

'Yep. Police. I'm in the police.'

The doc glances at Paul for a microsecond. 'Yes, well, I think the bit we should focus on is you usually take medication that helps you and we think maybe you haven't been taking it lately.'

'Mmm. Give me time to think.'

'Sure. All the time you need.'

The guy is ready to bolt, but then he just walks back towards the door into the hall that sits towards reception, outside the day room. The doc and the heavies let him walk past them, but then do a reverse ferret back out after him.

Five minutes pass. Maybe more, Paul isn't sure. Then it's a replay of the whole manoeuvre, except the chat has changed.

'So, this is the ward. You're in a mental health ward,' the guy is saying to the doctor.

'OK,' the doc replies.

'We think you haven't been taking your medication,' the guy says.

'Are you sure about that?' the doctor says.

'Yep,' says the guy. 'We, me and these gentlemen,' he indicates the heavies, 'We're quite concerned about you, frankly.'

'Is that right?' says the doc.

'Yep. Quite concerned. But you're OK now. We're here to help. These gentlemen and me, I'm a doctor, I'm showing you around.'

'Is that right?' the doc repeats.

'Yep,' says the guy. 'Just to get you settled in. But I'm really going to have to insist, after that, that you take your medication.'

'Are you sure it's me that needs the medication?'

'Yep, I'm a doctor,' the guy says, before heading back out the door.

Paul doesn't see this guy again during his stay; probably taken to the locked ward.

A young man is admitted overnight and spends his first hours in here not sleeping, screaming and thumping the window of his room. This is what everyone woke up to, if they got any sleep at all. Any minute it seemed the glass would break, or the nurses might make it stop. Please, God, make it stop.

Paul awakens with his heart thumping. Everything is thumping. The young man, the glass, Paul's heart. The walls seem to be thumping. The sky looks like it is thumping when he opens the curtains. Paul feels more fucked than any other day in here. Fucking fucked, like a drained cunt, tired, a tired fucking prick, he is, like if he needed a shit his arsehole couldn't muster the strength to squeeze it out. Like a worn-out whore, coming up forty, used in every hole, having to do pelvic exercises to pull in her hole so the man could feel his cock was inside something more than an open paper bag.

He stumbles into the walled enclosure, garden, whatever you want to call it, crouches down into a stress position by the wall, his arms up around the sides of his head. Still wearing his pyjamas. He doesn't mean to because there are other people around, but he farts loudly then says, 'Sorry,' to no one in particular. No one seems to have noticed. Sitting at a picnic bench are two of the mental, Paul's not sure of their names. One is eating porridge and the other is drinking coffee and smoking. Paul fetches his smoking gear from his pyjama trousers' pocket and lights up. His hands are shaking. He holds the cigarette in his hand and returns his arms to the side of his head. There's another couple of mental over by the outside wall, chatting and taking in the sunlight, which will creep across this wall as the day progresses. A day. Jesus, can he really make it for another day? Another day like *this*? Then the young man admitted last night comes out into the enclosure and asks Paul for a smoke, which Paul gives him and lights him up. The young man, who we'll all learn later has finally cracked after he wanted just to play his piano, in a band, say, but his parents had made him study to be a doctor instead, takes a long drag without touching the smoke with his hands and then spits it out towards Paul, who watches it fall to the ground a few feet from him. The young wants-to-play-piano-doesn't-want-to-be-a-doctor man then walks over to the mental at the picnic table and asks the one smoking for a roll-up, which he receives (the smoking mental has his back to Paul, didn't see what just happened), has lit for him, deep toke, and then spits out on the ground without ever touching it with his hand (his hands are clasped tight at the small of his back). The mental watches passively. Paul watches passively. Everybody is watching passively.

Paul walks into the ward to the kitchen and fixes himself some horrible instant coffee. When he walks back out to the enclosed garden, the young admitted-last-night-piano-not-doctor man has unclasped his hands and is making his way up the tree that sits in the middle of the garden area. It's more of a garden area than a garden per se, Paul is thinking. And an enclosure? That's like in a zoo, really. He's happier with his garden area description, more satisfied in his own mind that he has pinned down exactly what this *thing*, this *place*, is. He sits down with the other two mental, though of course he himself is not mental, as he's just in here suffering for some reason he can't quite remember just at the moment, suffering like a fucking prick, a fucking cock, a fucking arsehole, a fuck-ing cunt, and with the mental he is sat beside he watches as the young blah-blah-blah-piano-doctor man climbs higher into the tree and the mental facing him is saying something about something and just chatting away about being an A-MEEE-RICAN, A-MEEEEE-RICAN, an A-MEEEE-RICAN, do we see? Then the young blah-blah-blah-bladdeee-blah man, twenty feet up the tree, maybe, jumps off the branch he's on. The A-mee-rican turns and looks over and turns back and says something more about how, 'I'm American, but I'm me, so, you see, am an A-mee-rican,' and the other mental smokes and Paul takes a sip of his horrible coffee. The two mental chatting by the wall wander back into the ward and some nurses are coming out about the tree leap thing, we all sup-pose. 'Is that a mulberry?' one of the mental says. It might even have been Paul.

'I got to get out of here,' Paul whispers, to no one, once he has gathered his thoughts, an hour or so later.

2.11

Someone must have said something, because a few days before Paul's due to leave hospital, with orders to return to his parental home for another four weeks while a decision is taken about where he should now live, his birth name, which is Paul but not Dorian, is reported by the freelance journalist who is, by now, working for the *Independent*. Other details reported about Paul Thomson are the three years he spent as a police officer before his, Paul Thomson's, sudden disappearance off the face of the earth. About the same time a Paul Dorian started showing up at the offices and on the demonstrations of a tiny environmental group which had former links to a far-left protest group that had former links to Greenham Common nuclear demonstrators. The day that Paul leaves the hospital he expects to be confronted by a bank of photographers and journalists, jostling to move in on him. But out here it's silent, empty. He looks around himself almost in a daze, then starts to walk up to the bus stop at the top of the long drive out of the hospital grounds. He has to get to his parents' house. His parents are called Nancy* and Freddie.* They live about a hundred miles from here. He hasn't seen them in close on twenty years. As he gets to the end of the driveway of the hospital, he stops dead in his tracks. There, about fifty feet along from him on the main road, is their car. And in their car is Julia, Liv and Soph. A huddle of photographers and journalists he was expecting and they're absent. It's a trap, something he'll need an escapologist trick to get out of. Their car with his wife and kids inside he was not expecting and there they are. He looks back towards the hospital, looking as though he might turn back and walk back into the ward. But then he moves forward and gets into the front passenger seat. He looks around at the girls in the back seats – Soph is passed out sleeping, Liv is staring out of the window at her side and doesn't turn to look at him – and then he looks at his wife. No one has said anything. Julia turns the key in the ignition and the engine starts. She puts the clutch in and the car into gear. Paul is looking out of the side window, then out of the windscreen. 'Are you sure?' he says quietly. Revs increase as Julia's foot pushes lightly at the accelerator. 'Are they?' Paul says. And Julia lets the clutch out gently as her foot pushes down on the accelerator and the car begins to wheel forward and away from the kerb. Julia is concentrating on indicating and checking her mirrors and a glance over her shoulder. Maybe that's why she doesn't reply. They drive the sixty or so miles back to north London.

About thirty miles from home Soph wakes up and once she comes to she shouts, 'I spy! I spy! Conceptual I spy!' A game taught to her on other journeys in the car.

'I'll go first,' Julia says. 'I spy, with my little eye, something beginning with T.'

'Tension?' Liv deadpans.

No one says anything.

'Texture?' Soph says.

'Yes!' says Julia.

'Yeah. You've done that one before,' Soph says.

'Have I?' Julia says.

'OK,' Paul says, smiling back at Soph, 'your turn.'

'I spy, with my little eye, something beginning with... I,' Soph says.

'Intrigue?' Liv deadpans again.

'Nope,' Soph says.

'Iniquity?' Julia hazards.

'Nope,' Soph says.

'Injustice?' Paul tries.

'Yes!' Soph says, and starts laughing.

'What injustice are you thinking of?' Paul says.

'All of it,' Soph says, sweeping her right hand over the rolling fields of England, of Hertfordshire. 'All of them.'

'Brilliant,' Julia says, and she looks at Paul, smiles, then looks back at the road, with South Mimms services rapidly approaching.

'Your turn!' Soph says.

'OK,' says Paul, feeling he wants to jolly things along, washed clean by a free feeling, hanging himself on a comma, says, 'I, spy, with my little eye, something beginning with… F.'

'Um… flexibility?' says Julia.

'Nope,' says Paul. 'Your turn,' he says to Liv.

'I don't know,' says Liv. She shrugs. 'Freeways?'

'That's practically like something real,' says Paul. 'Soph, do you want to give it a go?'

'Something beginning with F…' Soph says. 'Something beginning with F… Freedom!'

Paul says, 'Wow. Now, that is amazing. Brilliant. Soph, you're a genius! Yes. Freedom.' He smiles. He looks at his wife. She's smiling, but watching the road. He turns. Soph is smiling.

About half an hour after they get back to the house there are twelve or so men and one woman with cameras and microphones out by the gate at the front of the house. Paul notices that the woman is not the Nosey from the pub. 'I always wonder,' Paul says as he's closing over the curtains in the front room, 'why do they stop there?'

'What?' Julia says. 'Who where?'

'Press. When they're doing these things,' Paul says. 'I mean, if they're just going to stand there, why don't they storm the door or something? Poke a microphone through the letterbox or something?'

'Duh,' Liv says, 'It would be against the law or something. Wouldn't it?' She looks anxiously at her mother.

'Oh yeah,' Paul says. 'Of course it would. They can't come in here.'

Taking a peek out from behind the closed curtains Julia says, 'Looks like we'll be living in the gloom for a few days.'

'Yeah,' Paul says. 'Looks like.'

Within the light of a lowered ceiling lamp above the dining-room table, Paul and Julia sit across from each other after the girls have both retreated to their bedrooms. 'I suppose you want to know stuff. What do you want to know?' Paul says.

'What do people ever want to know about other people?' Julia says. 'I suppose I should start with, why did you do it, Paul? But I'm not sure after twenty years that's really the right question.' She takes a gulp of her glass of wine. 'It should be something more like, can you remember back far enough and explain what the boy you were then was thinking? For all I know it was just a way to make a living.'

'You wouldn't be that far off in thinking that,' Paul says. 'And you're right. This is as far as I can remember it. Do you hate me? Do you hate who I was back then?'

Julia is smiling. 'You had a van, you know?' she says. 'You were so useful. Practically no one else could drive, let alone owned a vehicle. And you drove so safely.'

'They teach you defensive driving.'

'And you were always so practical in other ways, knew how to wire up a socket, do repairs to the van, that kind of thing, yet you always had those shiny shoes, looked after yourself. I should have known. You know, I fell in love with you the night you came over late and I had been trying to set up a new Excel sheet for membership of... what was it then? I can't remember exactly, but we were still with Bob and his lot then and you took over the work for me. You were just so sweet, turning up with that book, Excel 2000 or whatever year it was, and I was so freaked out. Remember the way we used to be at the dinner parties? Oh, cute. All too cute! When we were asked that time at a party as part of an ice breaker what the memoir of our relationship would be called, you said, "The Struggle for Dinner." If we couldn't think of anything much to say to who we'd just been introduced to, a Rob or an Abolanya or a Mark or an Ann, a

Lisa or an Emdad or Mahdi or Carlos, we used to joke about our chaotic existence, how we couldn't ever get it together, anything, the way we needed a website called Lastsecond.com – that Last-minute.com implied just a whole lot more forward planning than we could ever muster. I used to say, "He's into music, Captain Beefheart, and I'm into baking. Oh, and we're both trying to save the planet." It was sickening, really, don't you think? And that was all mostly before the girls came along. Then I'd say, "Oh, and we're both trying to save the planet for our kids." When I look back, now.' She shakes her head. Paul sits quietly, lifting a beer bottle to his lips to drink. 'I remember the time that Liv was talking about something and she had just learned that thing, "Happiness writes with white ink on white paper." "But is that right?" you said. Then you went into this whole thing, "Because that man who said that happiness writes white, well, a household like this one, a family like this, has to think that that man was a bad man, who devoted a whole tetralogy of novels to misogyny, a man who was a collaborationist, a reactionary, probably an anti-Semite." You were just so… passionate. You so wanted to get over to your daughter the way she had to see things for what they are. "You have to know your history," was a favourite of yours. "Take nothing on trust. Question things," you used to tell Liv. And even when your daughters shrug and say, "Hmm," and don't really raise their eyes, you still make the effort, still try to teach them the right values. You know I heard you recently with Liv and you were saying, "I hope you're on Wikipedia, questioning things, checking things," and then you said, "And then check the things on Wikipedia against Snopes!" And the way you make the girls watch the Channel 4 News. I love that in you, the care you put into trying to protect them from the stupid world.' Then Julia stops speaking and stops smil-ing. 'Can I ask,' she says, finally, 'Do you love your kids?'

'What kind of thing is that to say?' Paul says, then he winces. 'Of course I love my kids. Jesus, if I found it impossible to love anything else in the world, I would still love them. You must know that.'

'And, so, do you still want to go on living with us?' Julia says.

'Is that really possible? With our friends outside?' Paul says.

'I have a feeling,' Julia says, 'that the next scandal is just round the corner, and our friends trying to look and listen and fire questions in are going to evaporate soon enough. There aren't even that many of them out there.' She is smiling again. 'We're not royalty or celebs.'

'I don't know,' Paul says, and then it pains him to add, 'I might have orders.'

'Oh, bugger orders,' Julia says. 'That'll all be shot to pieces now, won't it? Won't it?'

'I'm not sure,' Paul says.

'Well, those buggers can know anything about me they want to know, I've got nothing to hide,' she says.

'To be honest,' he says, 'I've no idea why I've been kept hanging around for… any operational reasons. My reports have been the same repeated information since about the time Liv was born. I'm not even sure I am part of their operation any more. They just happen to pay me.'

'I always kind of wondered about your work and the People's Republic of Rock and Roll making you any money, let alone the amazing amounts that kept turning up regular as clockwork.'

'Yeah, well…'

'Well nothing. If they want to go on chucking money at you for knowing where our next march is going to be, when they could just find out by looking up our website, more fool them. Sod them.'

'And you really want me to go on living here with you and the kids?'

'Look, Paul, I'm not saying I'm not pissed off at you. I am. Or I am in retrospect, if you know what I mean. I'm pissed off at the young guy I met back then. The infiltrator. But I have to believe… I don't know. That we got together and then had kids and then got married in some sense because we are these people now. We've been the we that we are for too long now – let's just go on being that. I'm too tired to be anyone else.'

'You know what they're going to call you, don't you? And what they're going to call me?'

'Oh, bugger all that.'

'And your standing on the committee, and the exec? You've just been on your last march. No?'

'Why?' Julia says sharply. 'Certainly, if I had some undercover in my home, I'd be a liability. But I don't, do I? Not now. We all know who you are. The cause has our own little captive Met officer to teach in the ways of righteousness.'

'Yeah,' Paul says. 'Fair enough.'

'Anyway,' Julia says, 'It's late. Time for bed. You're officially in the doghouse for a while – at least, until we can sit down with the girls and try to explain to them the way we see things.'

'Yeah.'

'You're on the couch.'

'Yeah,' Paul says, 'Fair.'

2.10

On Saturday morning Julia says that she has to go into her office because of some sort of crisis in one of the refuge houses that the charity she works for runs. It will be the first time that Paul has been alone in the house with the girls. There's an awkward tension between all of them, visible in positions in the house and the looks on faces when they happen to come together. And Paul has become amazingly clumsy during these days, dropping a cup and a glass on the floor, miscuing a vinyl record on the turntable and scratching a deep groove into a Van Morrison record of Julia's. Only this morning, early, he came into the kitchen and almost fell into a dead faint into a set of wire shelves that have ladles and knives and pots and pans hanging from them and the clatter and bang stilled into a silence in which no one came to see what had happened to him. Julia walks out blithely towards the reporters, now down to two men, one with a camera and one with a large, Zeppelin-like microphone. 'Don't you feel violated?' the reporter says. We can plainly see this is in the hope of provoking her into saying something. But Julia opens and closes the gate and pushes past them. The cameraman and reporter turn towards her, but as she makes her way along the street they quietly turn back and stare forlornly at the curtained house again. Julia walks all the way to her office, two miles or more, and walks past the door of the offices, along an avenue which forks off to the left and into a Catholic church, where she meets a priest, who is sitting in a pew waiting for her.

'How are you, Julia?' he asks.

'It's hardly what I'd call been easy, Father Michael,' she says.

'No. No. I can imagine,' says the priest. 'You must feel mightily betrayed. Mightily betrayed.'

'Oh, it's not that,' Julia says. 'So my husband is a copper. More than a wee thing to overlook, for sure. But he's still him. Do you know what I mean, Father?'

'Of course. I understand fully,' Father Michael says. 'These must be mighty trying times for you. How are the girls?'

'Well, that's what I mean, Father. They're just... them. Moody or loud and screeching, but just them. And they think, oh, their father is just their father. You know, they're the age where parents couldn't be any uncooler, you know? Well, then one of them turns out to be in the police, and that probably is uncooler, but not by any order of magnitude to our terminal uncoolness. Do you see what I mean, Father Michael?'

'I do. I see it all. In a way it is good, Julia. You said on the phone that press people were outside the house. That must be a frightening experience for the girls.'

'I think they think it happens in everyone's life at some point or other, to be honest. Every celebrity in their world has been doorstepped. Every royal. Everyone, as far as they're concerned,' Julia says, and starts laughing. 'They just shrug. The younger one even likes running past them on the way to and from school. Like she's a celebrity because of this, now.'

'And your eldest – Olivia, isn't it? How does she cope?' says Father Michael.

'Oh. Well, she's refusing to go to school at the moment. That'll be the thing now probably till the holidays,' Julia says.

'Understandable. It must be difficult, very difficult for one so young.'

'Yes, Father.'

'Now. I know you wanted a wee chat and all that, but is there anything…? Do you want, perhaps, for me to hear your confession, Julia?'

'Yes, Father. I'd like that.'

'Of course. Of course. Not a problem in the slightest. Shall we…?'

'Yes, Father.'

2.9

On the Wednesday of the next week Paul tells Julia that he has to go into Scotland Yard. 'Probably to be chucked,' he says. It's going to take up his whole day. Back up to three press outside the front door now, but the twelve or thirteen have evaporated, like Julia said they would. Still, he goes out the back door of the house to the back-yard fence. There he calls out, 'Anybody there?' Then he scrambles over the fence into the lane that comes out in the next street that no one would suspect is connected with their house. He takes the Tube to Embankment (cameras 2, 12, 7B, 42, 1, 13, 9A, 7BC, 8FD, 72, 4, 6, #3, 7, 14,

12, 6, 9, 6YG, 27, A, B, 5, 1, 4, 7, 4, 3, 5, 2, 27, 5A, 7B, Front, Side, Back, 5, 13, 25, Backgate, 12, 4, 6, #9, #7, #1, f, ftdr, 4, 6, 8, 7), walks until he's past Victoria Coach Station (cameras FE, SE, BE, 6, 31, 22, 1, 3, 2, 1, FRONTGATE, 6, 5, 1, 3, 8, 6, 23, 13, 1, AB, CB, #5, #4, 2, 6, 3), takes the Tube to Piccadilly Circus (cameras 1, 4, No4, No3, No2, 3, 5, J, K, L, 2, 3, 7, 9, 3, X, XI, 4, SE, S, SW, 44, 32, 6), then loses himself in the crowd for a while before leaving the station. He walks to Scotland Yard (cameras Sideent, Backent1, Backent2, 3, 4, 2, 5, 1, 4, 6, 2, 7f, 7e, 7d), to a gate (a sign: Camera Enforcement In Operation, PIN numbered and ID card shown) and then a back door (cameras ██████████████). After he pushes the buzzer and enters after a response, he walks along a long corridor (cameras ████████), up three flights of stairs (cameras ████████), along another long corridor (cameras ████████), around a corner, then a short corridor (cameras ████████) and into a small, anonymous room which has a window into the corridor but no window to the outside world (camera ████). The guv'nor and the sarge are sitting across a table from him. The guv'nor signals for Paul to sit in a plastic chair in front of him. 'I suppose that's it, I'm out,' Paul says.

'Don't jump to conclusions, Paul,' the sarge says.

'How's that going to work?'

'We work round it,' says the guv'nor. 'Roll with the punches, fuckwit. You fucking Mock Jock. Protect the integrity of the operation.'

'Mock Jock. Mock Jock,' Paul says. 'Have you noticed everyone in the Met seems to be Scottish, or at least has Scottish parents?'

The sarge nods and says, '*Scotland* Yard,' then smiles.

'Nice,' Paul says.

'Look. What is undercover?' the guv'nor says. 'Does it mean that you have a watertight disguise? We're no playing at fucking dress-up, here, are we now? Officer?'

'No, sir.'

'It's no fucking fancy dress.'

'Sir.'

'Do you think you're at a masquerade party, a masked ball, mibby, constable?'

'Sir?'

'Are you out for Hallowe'en?'

'No.'

'Doing a bit of guising? Are you going to sing me a song, tell a wee joke? Do a wee turn?'

'No, guv.'

'Wake up, then. It's no about that, is it?'

'OK,' Paul says. 'What, then?'

'Knowing who we really are, that's what's what. So, you were a muesli and hummus-munching environmentalist hippy. Now you're a copper in one of those families. What's the difference, fuckwit?'

'Did you see what they called me in the papers? What they said about my wife and kids?'

'The papers? Look, I do care what goes in the rags. I care that they've something in there that is operationally useful. I like it when we've pushed our message down their fucking throats and it shites out all over the plebs. I do. I like it. It's just we have to assess. Who are you? If she's let you back in the house, I mean. For all we know that's how everyone's going to react if and when. Otherwise they look like fucking cunts, don't they?'

'This is never going to work.'

'Who says?'

'What do you really hope to achieve?'

'Whatever we can. That's all we can hope for.'

'I'm just not sure… Jesus. I just stay on living in there?'

'Well, add something to it, fuckwit. Tell a rag you want to expose the Met, what your bosses were up to. Say you're going to write a book about the whole sad, sorry fucking mess. What you were made to do, what you were made to say. Aye, I'm warming to this idea. What will we call the book?'

'No idea.'

'Something punchy. "Good Cop". Something like that. "This Good Cop".'

'Sure, why not?'

'Naw, wait. It has to be "It's a Fair Cop". Naw?'

'Naw.'

'I thought that was OK.'

'I'd like to see which fucking Noseys come out of the wood-work with which papers and what amount of money for the exclusive. That's some real intel I could be doing with. And as for the other thing. Tell them you stayed under for the twenty-odd years because you were slowly and subtly changing your mind. Your mind has been expanded. You see it all now. You see everything. You have heard the word, and the word is good. The message has got to you. The hippies are right on the money. Only they can save the world with their lefty politics and a good old demonstration down Whitehall.'

'And what do I tell my wife? My kids?'

'Same. You have become the Paul they know. You're going to tell them the Met keep dragging you in to twist your melon, but you're going to be talking to the rags, are you not? You're going to be writing a book about the shits who made you do it. You're going to bury those fuckers. Oh, and tell your wife you love her, always have. Tell your kids...' The guv'nor looks at Paul. 'I don't know, I'll leave that one to you.'

'Fucking hell,' Paul says, sitting back and rubbing the sides of his head. It's like he's trying to wake himself up. 'What the fuck is this all *for?*' he says.

'Because we're right,' the guv'nor says without hesitation. 'Because *it* is necessary. You think we can just let people go around doing and thinking and saying what they fucking well please? What kind of policing operation would we be then? What kind of police *force*? We're fucking bobbies, we're… what do they call us up north?'

'Polis?'

'Obviously I know that one. Christ! I mean in like Liverpool.'

'Bizzies?'

'Bizzies, that's it, that's the one I was thinking. I'm a busy man myself.'

Paul stops rubbing his brow and sighs. 'Come on,' he says, 'there's been ones we've all disagreed with, had bad feelings about.'

'Which?'

'Well, what Lewis was doing in with the black family. Can't say that was right.'

'The Lawrences?'

'I still never use their name. I always just think, like we used to say, the black family. After that I said I for one didn't want to do any more black family cases. That's why I avoided the Menezes thing.'

'You couldn't know there were going to be more. How did you know there were going to be more?'

'Come on, guv'nor.'

'Anyway. That was a protection. The shite was never going to be used.'

'Oh yeah?'

'Well, it wasnae, was it? No really.'

'Only because there was nothing. Nothing to work with. Nothing to dig up. Jesus. Sometimes, and I'm not saying all the time, but sometimes, we are the filth. When I saw him in the background, at one of the meetings, on the telly. Jesus. I thought, we can't be, can we? I was that naïve.'

'Look, you choose whose side you are on. We all do. And we've been on the right side, I can tell you that, fuckwit, for nothing.'

'Maybe.'

'Not maybe. Definitely. Look. You're Paul Thomson. You're one of the Met's finest. You're a good copper. You've done good for your nation. You're a hero. You're hot fuzz. Nation loves you. You keep us safe. You protect the nation. You love the Queen and she fucking loves you back. Got it?'

Paul looks up and Fabius is standing by the door into the room. The guv'nor and sarge look around. 'Hello, Thomson,' Fabius says. Paul looks silently from the guv'nor to Fabius.

Finally, the guv'nor says, 'Forgive him, he had no idea you knew his name, who the fuck he was.'

'That's fine. Well, we're always best when we're at our most anonymous. Isn't that so, Thomson?'

Paul manages a shrug of acknowledgement, a nod. Fabius is looking around the room. 'Safe comes first in "Building a safe, just and tolerant society." I was just thinking the other day about Maggie's words, remember, way back in the Greenham Common days? "To those who want us to close down the American nuclear bases in this country, let me say this. The cost of keeping tyranny at bay is high, but it must be paid. The threat of the Soviet Union is ever present and it's growing continually."' Another glance at each of them in turn. 'Good, well, carry on,' Fabius says. 'Remember what we're in it for, Thomson. Because we're in the right. Because we are necessary.' And with a return nod, Fabius is gone.

The sarge says, 'Say I'm tripping if you like, but I think Fabius just did the voice, and pretty accurately, quoting Maggie.'

'Right,' says the guv'nor, 'you need some reminding. Sarge?'

Paul sits back and breathes deeply. He blinks a few times, clearing his eyes. 'Um, sure, yeah,' he says.

The sarge – who is wearing civvies, by the way, a pair of jeans, a wild-patterned shirt and Clarks deep-blue suede desert boots – says, 'So, someone has blundered. Well, now, what a privilege. I get to drill an actual celebrity.'

'I didn't *try* to get into the rags,' Paul says.

'But you got there, sonny boy. That was remiss. Still, not the end of the world.' The sarge walks over to a drawer and starts searching through electronic equipment in there.

'So now I've got a drilling on being a good copper, have I? A few policies and procedures, is it?'

'What?' says the sarge. 'What made you think that?'

'Just, the guv'nor was saying… I've got to remember who I am.'

'Naw. I want to do a Beefheart pop quiz. Keep you on your toes.'

'What? Really?'

'If you change too much, well, that could fuck it all, couldn't it?'

'What's not fucked? Everything is fucked.'

'Shite. Naw. You're still in the house, are you not? You're still in the Met, are you not? We just have to be more careful about contact is all. It's good, actually. You're out of the Met, you're going to whistle-blow, write a book, exposé, full gory details, shite like that. The full *News of the Screws* transsexual vicar, cocaine binge hooker shitestorm of shitery. But we'll know the truth. That's right, is it not, Paul?'

After this, the guv'nor stands, nods, turns, leaves.

Paul turns to the sarge. 'But we can change some stuff, right? I don't have to continue the label, do I?'

'What? Get woke, sonny boy. Actually, I've got another ten grand for you. I'll get it in a bit. Remind me before you go.'

'But…'

'But nothing. You cannot change too much. It will fuck the whole thing. In fact, do the thing. Get the cards out.'

Paul pulls a deck of cards out of his pocket and shuffles them and throws down three on the table. The sarge picks one. Paul says, 'Six of hearts.' The sarge turns it over and it is the six of hearts.

The sarge says, 'Tell me this time.'

2.9

'Nah. Look. This whole thing *is* fucked. You don't understand, the crazies I have to hang out with for that. Fucking Stewart and the rest of them. They give themselves Beefheart *names*. You have to see my plight. I have a guitarist called Nut Bolt Gourd and a sound engineer called Fumbalina. There's Cee Dee Steve and Pat the Knife—'

'Don't care. It's… it's kind of like the Pranksters thing. They had names.'

'You have to understand. They call me Wilkorn K. Passageway. I mean what does *that* even *mean*? And what will they come up with now they know I'm a copper?'

'We can't fix that right now.'

Paul has raised his hands like he's pleading with the sarge. The sarge looks him up and down saying nothing, then, 'Shall we get going? I like a bit of a cavort.'

'A what?' Paul says.

'I said I like a bit of a cavort… Naw? I don't *like* music. *Performance*. The film. Mick Jagger. Naw? If you hin't seen it, sonny boy, you need to.'

'Mick Jagger? Music movie? Hippy movie, is it?'

'Dirty movie. A critic – there's a scene with Mick in the bath – said even the bathwater was dirty.'

'Ha.'

'It is a sort of dirty hippy movie, but all smashed together with a London gangster flick. Classic. James Fox. I like a bit of a cavort.'

'Sounds like a Mick Jagger line. He was always cavorting.'

'Old rubber lips? Actually, it hin't Jagger that says that line, it's James Fox.'

'And it's good, this film? Is Jagger any good in it?'

'Well,' says the sarge, 'I heard he was asked just to play himself. But then that didn't seem to work out. Nic Roeg says to him, "You're just not convincing at playing Mick Jagger." After that Jagger starts playing Keith, and that went much better, apparently.'

'Sounds about right,' Paul says.

'Yeah, it's good. Got some silly bloody accents in it for the gangsters, though, fucking hell.'

'Yeah?'

'Seen that film, um, *The Lives of Others*?' the sarge says.

Paul throws his hands up. 'Nah.'

'Should do. It's good. I got it on DVD. They're great, them things. Extras. Extra features. On this one, there's a short film with all this Stasi pieces of kit.'

'Is that what it's about?'

'What's what about? The film, you mean? Aye, East Germany, you know, the Stasi. German Democratic Republic. It's very *The Conversation*, you know? That Frank Coppola movie. Gene Hackman. Brilliant. So, anyway, this Stasi kit, just amazing. Must have been well ahead of their time. Making things little and all that. You see a mic next to a fucking match, you know, a safety match, a thing for lighting your ciggies. And then there's this surveillance camera they used, and fuck me if it hin't almost exactly like the ones we still use now. All going round and round on this little hexagonal table to display everything. I really enjoyed it.'

'That would be an interesting one,' Paul says.

'What would be an interesting what?' says the sarge.

'I was just wondering while you were saying, I wonder how many cameras are in London now in comparison to the number of cameras in East Berlin back then? Or even the whole of East Germany?'

'German Democratic Republic.'

'Yeah, I wonder how many cameras are in London right now in comparison to the German Democratic Republic back then? Sarge?'

'Aye, I get what you're saying,' says the sarge.

'Yeah,' says Paul.

'Well, we're not the fucking Stasi, are we? We're not oppressive. We're… Well, remember we're a police *force*. We're a… a…'

'What? What are we, sarge?'

'Cautious. And we've been courteous. Now it's time to be... Aye, OK, I get your point.'

'Well, you're the philosopher, sarge, aren't you? You're the wise man on the mountain.'

'I am all that, your genuine Scots polymath,' says the sarge, and puffs out his chest. He's the fine figure of a man when he can be arsed. 'But, having said that, I have been reading a lot more Genette recently than, say, Foucault. No really up on my philosophy of freedom just at the mo.'

'Genette?' Paul says. 'Who's he at home?'

'Oh, brilliant. Frenchman. Gérard Genette. All about how a story gets told, who this and that are in and out of the narrative.'

'Sounds a bit heavy, sarge.'

'Heavy? Naw. It's a scream. He takes Propp's work on myths, looks how you can rip them up and see them different ways once you have the language to do so, *and* once you've cottoned on to what's being done to you as a reader or a viewer or a listener or a whatever. You seen that film, *Five Easy Pieces?*'

'Yeah. Jack Nicholson, right?'

'Correct. I been investigating that one. See, in the film, Jack plays his sister-in-law some piece on the old Joanna, and when she says it is just beautiful music and beautifully played, well, he sniggers. She asks why he's sniggering and he says—'

'He played it because it was the easiest piece he could think to play.'

'Spot on. So, right, then the film is called *Five Easy Pieces*. So, I'm thinking, these two things are linked, you know? Easy pieces, and five of them. I watched it a fair few times now, and at first I'm thinking, there must be five easy pieces of music in the film. Didn't exactly get very far with that. I don't know enough about classical music, I reckon. Need to get a scholar in on that, some intel, you know? Hang on, you don't know anything about classical music, do you?'

Paul shakes his head.

'Aye, too much to hope for, really. So, anyway, reading Genette I got a new theory, din't I? That the director and writers, they're saying the film *itself* is made up of five easy pieces. Of cinematic genres or something. You know, the hippy road movie, the high society family drama, the blue-collar roustabout, that sort of thing. Except it depends how you break it down, din't it? Have to admit, I hin't got too far with that yet either.'

'Certainly seems to make you able to see further, sarge.'

'You read *Ways of Seeing*, lad called Berger?'

'No.'

'Well, anyway. Next time you're talking to a scrote, and they're giving it all that, what with keeping Genette in mind, you just see right through what they're on about, where they're coming from, and most of all – most of all! Dah dah dah! – what they're fucking trying to hide.'

'Don't think I'm quite up to applying all the philosophy stuff the way you do.'

'No one is, sonny boy.'

'I know.'

'You seen that film, *Solaris*?'

'George Clooney?'

'Naw, pal. The Russian version. Tarkovsky, hin't it?'

'I've seen the George Clooney one.'

'It's all right. But the Russian one's better.'

'So what about it? What's the theme of that one you want me to notice?'

'What? Naw, pal, I just like it.'

'Watch this one, sarge,' Paul says, and he pulls the deck of cards back out. He shuffles with some croupier moves (a riffle with a ripple and bridge; a butterfly ripple, no bridge; shows the sarge the faces of the cards with a ripple spread and a domino wave; it's during a final two splits that he does the thing) and deals two to the sarge.

'OK,' the sarge says. 'You been practicing those, boy?' Paul keeps his poker face. The sarge stares him straight in the eye. 'Aye, thought so,' he says, then turns his cards over, a Queen of hearts and an Ace of spades. 'Heh, twenty-one. OK.'

'Yeah, but watch this,' Paul says, and deals the five cards from the top for himself then turns them over.

The sarge is counting. 'Eighteen,' he says. 'I'd say do it again, but I suspect you can do it every time.'

Paul nods.

Then, finally, the sarge sighs, starts the CD player he's been fiddling with and *Trout Mask Replica* comes crashing in, a welter of discordant noise. 'Right, let's go over it again... Track?'

''When Big Joan Sets Up'.'

'Who are we listening to?' the sarge says.

'Magic Band.'

'Who?'

'Captain Beefheart and the Magic Band.'

'*The* Magic Band?'

'His Magic Band. *His* Magic Band. I'm still foggy from the fucking drugs. They were only styled *The* Magic Band on later releases, and now Don's dead I suppose the power struggle for His or The is dead, too.'

'Nice use of Don, there. You still in mourning?'

'It means more to me than even the shit I've recently been put through.'

'Shite. Naw. Anyway, when I said who are we listening to, I meant what's the classic line up?'

'Van Vliet, Harkleroad, Cotton, French and Boston. And Hayden.'

'Band names.'

'Captain Beefheart. Zoot Horn Rollo. Um. Antennae Jimmy Semens. Drumbo, obviously. And... Rockette Morton. And The Mascara Snake.'

'Right. Aye. Good. Very good. Right, let's listen to 'Frownland' again,' the sarge says, pressing the button to cue up 'Frownland'.

'Jesus,' Paul says. There's a sound of weary resignation in his voice. Can you hear it?

'What's up?'

'I had a funny experience with 'Frownland' when I was inside.'

'Eh?'

'On the wards.'

'Aye. Well. Naturally.'

2.8

When it's over and Paul leaves Scotland Yard, he decides to walk home and starts winding through streets until he finds himself in Cambridge Circus in Bloomsbury. He's standing at the corner, just as the street runs down to Shaftesbury Avenue, when a siren sounds, close, an ambulance bears down on him and he steps back on to the pavement looking up and to his right. The pavement, the kerb, there, here. Cambridge Circus materialises around him like a conjuring trick. Cambridge Circus, London, the buildings, that theatre, spring up around him. The buses, a car, two, three, halt at a junction on a green. Then people, the people, these people, London teeming with people, everywhere, in motion and at rest. Those people there, there, over there, here, there and there. How he spends his life in the bubble of his own consciousness, his self. When he first came to London, as he zigzagged erratically in the Tube or came to a stop on Oxford Street, people would walk right into him as though he simply wasn't there, or as though they did not want to deviate one centimetre from the line they took on their commute every working day of their lives because this would be to lose time, miss the Tube that gets them home at 5.27 rather than at 5.54. Teeming London. The people lining up along the pavement over there. The people almost here. The two people outside the shop across the way. The group of people over by the theatre. He steps back again, almost joining the group of people behind him, steps forward again then again because of the four, five, six people making their way across Cambridge Circus and into Shaftesbury Avenue. Then he watches as a bus passes and there are all the people in there, two faces at the top deck windows, the three people together at the back, the lone person up near the driver. And a car and the two people in the driver and passenger seats. The woman there with the two toddlers. The site workers lined up along the pavement over there. The group of students here. The two people outside the shop across the way. The teacher and the pupils over by the theatre. The man walks back into his shop and the other man walks away. His sight swarmed with people. The three site workers smoking and the fourth and fifth drinking cans of Coke. The man with the cigar changing direction and heading back towards the shop door. The teacher by the theatre handing out pieces of paper to the six pupils in her charge. The woman with the toddlers pulling them close to her as they prepare to cross the road. The students, four young women, one young man and one you could not be sure. And say for the sake of argument you knew the names of each. Mrs Baker, Ms Ballin, Mr Fletcher, Mr Adenuga, Ms Copeland, Mr Green, Mr Lodge, Ms O'Sullivan, Mr Lind, Ms Brown, Mrs Mews, Ms Tate, Mrs Woods, Mrs Wyatt, Ms Mensah, Mr Shanti-I, Ms Bailey, Mrs Richardson, Ms Bendeth, Mr Brown, Ms Bennett, Mr Colley, Ms Butler, Ms Deacon, Ms Conway, Mr Dean, Ms Abel, Mr Doherty, Ms Faith, Ms Shaw, Mr Harper, Mr Harrison, Ms Hennell, Mr Hill, Ms King, Mrs King, Mr King, Lord Lowe, Ms McCourt, Ms Samuels, Ms Lloyd, Mr MacDougal, Ms McLean, Mr Booker, Ms Agyeman, Mr Meyer, Mrs Moore, Ms Mwamwaya, Mr Nelson, Ms Macrae, Mrs Raworth, Mrs Schultz, Mrs Sirtis, Mr Reid, Smee, Ms Tandy, Mrs Whiteread, Ms Westerby, Mr Ritchie, Ms Smith, Mr Smith, Ms Maugham, Mrs Fielding, Mr Fielding, Mr Fielding, Ms Fielding, Mr Smith, Mrs Smith, Mr Borlase, Ms Dance, Mr Hardwick, Ms Litvinoff, Mrs Litvinoff, Ms Vanessa Bendeth, Mr William Brown, Ms Mary

Anne Bennett, Mr Vincent Colley, Ms Jacqueline Butler, Ms Catherine Deacon, Ms Emma Conway, Mr Alexander John Dean, Ms Eileen Abel, Mr Bernard Doherty, Ms Emily Lee, Ms Madelaine Shaw, Mr Harry Harper, Mr Harry Harrison, Ms Sara Hennell, Mr Charles Hill, Ms Sarah King, Mrs Sarah King, Mr John King, Lord Edward Lowe, Ms Marie McCourt, Ms Rebecca Samuels, Ms Nicola Lloyd, Mr Douglas MacDougal, Ms Fiona McLean, Mr David Booker, Ms Freema Agyeman, Mr Jacob Meyer, Mrs Gwyneth Moore, Ms Esau Mwamwaya, Mrs Helen Banks Baker, Ms Elizabeth Geraldine Ballin, Mr John Michael Fletcher, Mr James Joseph Adenuga, Ms Marion Louise Copeland, Mr Derek William Green, Mr John William Lodge, Ms Katherine Anne O'Sullivan, Mr John Corbyn Lind, Ms Suan Brown, Mrs Alison Theresa Mews, that man and woman moving too fast in their car in the traffic when the traffic is moving to think who they might be, and the man behind them and the four men behind them, Ms Brenda Wireko Tate, Mrs Amanda Justice Woods, Mrs Margaret 'Midge' Wyatt, Ms Katarina Mensah, Mr Ata Abu Shanti-I, Ms Imogen Margaret Anne Bailey, Ms Aiko Kaneko, Ms Chiharu Nishimura, Ms Ryoko Takeuchi, Ms Sakurako Maeda, Mrs Joanne 'Jo' Richardson. And also Mr John Wilson, Mr Józef Teodor Konrad Korzeniowski, Mr Kimitake Hiraoka, Mr Brian Ó Nualláin, Mr George Peretz, Ms Howard Allen Frances O'Brien, Mr Lev Davidovich Bronstein, Mr Vladimir Ilyich Ulyanov, Mr Ioseb Besarionis dze Jughashvili, Mr François-Marie Arouet, Mr Eric Arthur Blair, Mr Theodor Seuss Geisel, Mr Georges Prosper Remi, Mr Charles Lutwidge Dodgson, Mr Samuel Langhorne Clemens, Mr John Griffith Chaney, Mr Christopher Murray Grieve, Mr James Leslie Mitchell, Mr James Macpherson, Mr Roman Kacew, Mr Roman Kacew, Mr Ricardo Eliécer Neftalí Reyes Basoalto, Mr Samuel (or Samy) Rosenstock, Mr Tomáš Sträussler, Mr David John Moore Cornwell, Ms Qualcuno Nessuno, Mr Stephen Edwin King, and Mr Allan Stewart Konigsberg. Not forgetting Leah Hanwell, Felix Cooper, Natalie Blake and Nathan Bogle. Jo Richardson is on the top deck of a bus looking at Midge Wyatt and says sotto voce and to herself, to her phone but not talking on her phone, 'Gold boots, I don't *think* so,' and shakes her head; Alison Mews talks quietly to herself saying, 'What are these girls wearing? Where do they get their ideas?'; John King says, 'Can you believe this?', but his wife and daughter didn't hear because they have wandered further up the street than he had thought; Harry Harper is saying, 'Oh,' to no one; 'Wow, I thought it was on that side of the road,' says Elizabeth Ballin to herself; Jacob Meyer is talking to a colleague on his phone and he's saying, 'I can't get into it that way – you need to ask Jonathan; hold on,' and takes his phone from his ear to look at it briefly; Aiko Kaneko, Chiharu Nishimura, Ryoko Takeuchi and Sakurako Maeda are all talking apparently at the same time; James Adenuga is in conversation with Mari Copeland; Gwyn Moore and Esau Mwamwaya are talking to each other but they do not know each other; Alex Dean and Eileen Abel talk in low voices to each other; Marie McCourt, Bec Samuels and Nicky Lloyd throw back their heads laughing at something Bec just said; Mary Anne Bennett and Vince Colley talk to each other as colleagues and co-workers; Gwyn Moore goes on to talk to Freema Agyeman; Eileen is telling Alex, 'I wasn't happy about it in the first place and every day seems to get harder,' and Alex says, 'I wish I could... I wish I could say something to make you feel better,' and Eileen says, 'Don't worry about it so much, honestly,' and makes a move to walk away; Jim is saying to Mari, 'I just love it, it's so cool, mental,' and Mari smiles; Marie, Bec and Nicky can't talk for laughing. Alex thinks Eileen might be thinking about her situation all the wrong way, that she's really unhappy and he doesn't know what to do; Mari is thinking that Jim thinks he's God's gift to humanity but that his motives are always good and pure; he likes pleasing people, nice guy; Marie, Bec and Nicky are all thinking in strange synchronicity that each of the other two are thinking that it's just so great to meet up, though each are also thinking that they can't seem to elude their own individual problems; Nicky worries about her mother, Bec her husband and Marie herself; Midge is thinking these are the best boots ever, springy and a great colour, so happy; Smee is thinking about their degree dissertation; Gwyn Moore is thinking that she still doesn't know what part of London she is in after asking these two ladies; Eileen is thinking of Alex, he's only trying to help, let him, tell him; Vince is thinking that Mary is a really great co-worker and colleague and always ready with the right answer and Mary is thinking that Vince is a top quality arsehole – that cologne, uh, and always flashing that watch, Tag Hauer big balls; Midge is wondering where the young girls get these huge hoop earrings they are wearing and about her husband, who died four years ago, almost to the day; and Marie is thinking about the diagnosis she got last week... but now is not the right time – she thought it was but it's not; and Nicky is thinking about her devastating news about her marriage, but she'll leave it for now; and Alex is thinking, really, you know, I could be doing without this, but I can't tell her; and Mary is thinking London is teeming with people; and Gwyn is thinking London is teeming with people; and Jim is thinking, this place is ready to ignite, man, you know what I mean?; and Midge is thinking, London! London! London!; and Gwyn is thinking that she needs to ask a *white* woman where she is; and Eileen is thinking that London is teeming with people, so many people; and Esau is thinking, London gets me down sometimes; and Jim is thinking, London gets me down sometimes when I think this way; and Jo is thinking, will this bus ever move, ever?; and Gwyn is starting to feel scared; and Alex is starting to feel concerned as he suddenly imagines finding Eileen's dead body, just her dead body, not where or when this will be or is, that's all blank; and Freema is thinking, these people, honestly, I have to laugh; and Aiko, Chiharu, Ryoko and Sakurako are thinking amazingly similar thoughts about the culture shock of being in London and how when everything is this unfamiliar it also feels dangerous and they all think about each other that they are clutching their backpacks in such similar ways like an assault is waiting around every corner, but then that's the way with coming all this way; and Eileen is thinking, I could do, but I won't, but I could, but I won't; and Midge thinks, I should be going, getting out of here – it doesn't particularly feel safe; you can't ever tell in London, now, can you?; and Jo suddenly almost feels the imagined blast from below her on the lower deck, almost like a physical sensation, and reassures herself it's just that old feeling that she thought had died down over the last few years and nothing like 2006 – she wouldn't ride the buses again in 2005, but made a New Year's resolution because, come on, it was getting ridiculous – and anyway (let's face it) they could go off in the street or in the Tube or in a tall building or anywhere really and OLLI – is that it? Or was it OLLO or LOLO? One life: live it – sure she'd seen it somewhere – but it would be too hard to OLLIF, one life: live in fear; OOLLIFFI: only one life: live in fear for it; Oh, stop it, stop it, stop it; and Alex just feels so syrupy suddenly and all he wants is to get away; and Eileen thinks, just go if you have to; and all these people have a baseline of thinking that they are very, very unhappy and sad and tired and burdened but all can think, buck up, it's just London, it's a tiring place, even to just get around; and Jo Richardson still feels the weird abyss of the floor just having risen up in a blast and there being an almighty hole in the floor now and her scattered limbs and the wounds and the blood and the pain, oh Jesus, the pain, searing, sheer, unbearable, and even if she lives she'll be... Oh! It was unthinkable, unthinkable, unthinkable! And Joanna 'Jo' Richardson thought about her job and her family, Mrs Joanna 'Jo' Richardson, and her commute and the man on the Clapham Omnibus and omnishambles, her first day in the job as a minister and the name of the actress Rebecca Front, I love her, and the walk from the bus stop to home, and home and feet up and a cup of tea, nice. But there's just too much to know, Paul thought, if you want to know what people are doing and saying and you even want to know what people are think-ing. How much information would that all be? There's just too much. What are you looking for then? The thought that says, if the place goes up, I'll be on the streets with a Molotov cocktail, a brick, anything that comes to hand. Windows smashing? Fires burning? The woman on the top deck of the bus sighed; the person looked down from the bus not moving and saw the man, this other person, walking along. The four officers stopping and searching the black boy. Paul walks away through the throng feeling free, feeling the need to get a drink, maybe in that pub there, feeling the need to urinate. He passes the bus and the Japanese girls and the couple and the three women, these people, and these people, and these other people. Teeming London. Freedom is being able to piss, he thinks. When he was on the wards he always felt he needed to piss, but every time he went for one, it just wouldn't come, wouldn't flow easily. Something stopped. Stoppered. He tried thinking about Douglas, but that complicated matters. He would breathe, and breathe again, and sigh, and in then slowly out and count back-wards from seventeen. It seemed the first complicated enough num-ber to start from. Ten nine eight just too simple, too familiar, from rocket launches and stuff like that, and three two one was like a get set go that was too alarming, like waiting for the firing gun. So, seventeen sixteen fifteen was the one. Seventeen, sixteen, fifteen, um, fourteen, thirteen, eleven, I mean twelve, eleven, ten, nine, eh.

His piss would start to trickle out apologetically around about eight.

Eightish.

3.1

Back at the dining room table that evening, late on, beer and wine, they're laughing quietly. Then Julia says, 'What about the politics, Paul? Did you ever care?'

'I hated it when it was all and just about climate,' Paul says. 'Not because I think the science is bad or wrong or because there's not a catastrophe going on. It's just I couldn't stomach the way concern went up and up among the self-serving middle-class wankers we were protesting with. I mean, I really am the working-class boy you think I am. I'm not James Bond or anything. No dinner jacket, you know? The closer it got to home the more the whole world had to do something, the SJWs would be screaming. The whole world. What did they know about the whole fucking world? Hadn't they noticed that it was mostly the whole fucking world that had been suffering the consequences of even a not superheated whole fucking world's climate for fifty, sixty, hundreds of years, probably. I have this early memory… Biafra, or at least I remember watching *The Comedians* on TV and I certainly remember there being Biafran jokes. How funny it was they were starving to death! How many Biafrans were needed to tip the scales at seven stone, that sort of thing. And then, I don't know everything about world politics, but I know it's not pretty. Jesus, all you have to be is a fan of George Harrison or even Bob fucking Geldof to know that the world has been dropping like flies, drowned in Bangladesh, fried in Ethiopia, victims of their climates, and for years. If we had kind hearts, we should have sent death squads to finish them off quickly, instead of the lingering, hopeless deaths they had to suffer.' He stops and looks at Julia again. 'Sorry, that's going too far.'

'No,' says Julia. 'It's the same old passion. Whatever it stems from, I can still admire that it burns.'

'The stuff we had to see when it was animal rights. Fuck, when I get my PTSD from all this it'll be from those things we looked at rather than the double life – those groups have no fucking hearts.' Paul lowers his head and raises it again quickly. 'I liked trampling the GM crops. That had a bit of fun to it. And I liked it when it was hunt sabotage. I was particularly active in actions then, pushing for them. Because I wanted to spoil the fun, get at the hoorays. Didn't care much about the little furries, though nobody wants to see an animal suffer, do they? It was just such a fucking joy to get in the way of countryside wankers. But then we had to move along from that one, cause we won.'

'I wouldn't be so sure the wankers aren't getting around any ban. They always win.'

'Yeah. That's why the one I always can get into is the money one. I'm a, you know, a copper, not a landowner. Not a lord of the manor or anything. That Occupy Wall Street, that's the one I'm most interested in. There's moves for an Occupy London, aren't there? We should be part of that.'

'And Scotland Yard are going to put up with that, are they?'

'They chucked me. And anyway, it's like with the Beefheart.'

'Huh? I assume you aren't actually a fan?'

'I wasn't much, no. But that's what I mean. It's strange, but at some point of listening to the music over and over, and I mean the discordant noise, it was the sweet melodious stuff that became, well, less interesting. Almost... what's the word? Offensive. Unlistenable, really. Unlistenably musical. When a harmony floated in just the way it should into a guitar solo... it was like being force-fed ice cream. Tubs and tubs of ice cream. Sweet and sickening. I scream for crow, right enough. But it just wouldn't hold together.'

Julia looks at him quizzically.

'I mean, remember the year we met? The CPGB was just being dissolved and everyone was looking for homes. Democratic Left, Revolutionary Democrats, Socialist Workers. So unreal. Christ, in 1992, Ken Livingston said every single member of what was left of the CPGB was MI5!'

'I can kind of believe that,' Julia says.

'And then there was Socialist Labour, Socialist Alliance, Alliance for Workers' Unity. All that stuff until Respect, and then that falls apart into the Socialist Alliance Democracy Platform, Reds, the Marxists, New Workers, the Convention. They just couldn't hold it together.'

'Your fault?'

'You give me too much credit,' Paul says, smiling and dropping his head. Two minutes pass in silence.

'What about the label — what happens with that now?' Julia says. 'Are they going to keep paying you?'

'Actually,' and Paul raises his eyebrows and starts laughing, 'they gave me another ten big ones.'

'You are kidding!' Julia says and joins him laughing. 'Check you, flash! Mugs. Stupid buggers. What do you think they're getting out of this?'

'I do not know,' Paul says. 'Maybe it's their idea for disrupting... something. Launch more fucking God-awful Beefheart-inspired music into society.'

They both laugh and try to supress laughing and laugh all the more for trying to supress it.

'I always knew you hardly worked at all, that PR3 was more like a weekend hobby. And your job, the long lunch breaks — by three in the afternoon you'd disappear for the school run after you must have turned up at ten thirty because of your morning run.'

'I was working hard. Just not on that,' Paul says.

Julia looks at him and Paul drops his head again. Another few minutes of silence, then Julia says, 'You know, I always knew there was something wrong with you. Something fundamental.'

'Yeah?' Paul says, still smiling. Then the smile fades from his face.

Then Julia looks him over and says, 'Do you remember that time we were at a party and when we got home I said to you, "What the hell was that?" Do you remember?'

'What?' Paul says. 'What party?'

'The night, the party with... We got home from this party. A few years back. When Sophie was five or six. I said to you, "You tonight, singing that disgusting song." Remember? And you said, "What song?" And I said, "I heard you, across the room.

Disgusting. I couldn't believe it." Then you were like, "I can't even remember." And I said, "You were singing a disgusting song about Madeleine McCann. I can't believe you could stoop so low. It's just fucking disgusting." I was coming over like a right... And you were all jittery and confused. Then you said, "Madeleine... I was singing 'I've had zouzands of men, again and again...' By Madeline—" And I was like, "My God! Don't repeat it! You and those awful fucking people... fucking men giggling away. Jesus. Do you realise what you were singing? Do you realise how disgusting?" And you said, "I was singing a song from *Blazing Saddles*, the Mel Brooks movie, sung by Madeline *Kahn*, called 'I'm Tired', where she sings 'I've had zouzands of men, again and again, man, I'm tired...' You thought I was singing about Madeleine *McCann*? Jesus Christ." And I was saying, "You were singing... You were singing what? What do you mean?" Do you remember?' Paul says nothing. It looks like he's almost smiling. Put it down as, *Paul says nothing but smiles sadly*. 'And you told me again, to get it through my thick skull, "I was singing a comic song, from *Blazing Saddles*, by Madeline *Kahn*. Jesus." Jesus indeed. And I was saying, "Oh. Jesus. I thought you were... I don't know. It seemed like the kind of callous joke that men... that kind of sick joke that men... tell."'

'Mmm.'

'Do you remember?'

'I remember,' Paul says. 'Jeez, just like the Queen tribute thing.'

'The thing is,' Julia says, 'I don't think I've ever stopped thinking of you that way, you know? As the kind of arsehole who might have been telling a sickening joke, singing as Madeleine McCann. Do you know what I mean?'

Paul says nothing but smiles sadly.

3.2

On a Thursday Paul, almost for old times' sake, follows Julia off Holloway and on to Seven Sisters. She walks up into Finsbury and the crowds on the street thin out, so he keeps well back. But she's moving at pace and without looking around her, on a real mission to get to wherever she's going. It'll be a meeting with the Finsbury Park chapter. Whenever she goes on one of these ambles it's always a house that matches the list in the end. She checks her phone and heads down a street called Alexandra Grove. He waits at the corner of Seven Sisters, watching her slow then turn second left. He runs along, crosses Adolphus Street or Road, he only catches sight of the name, a worn and tattered older street sign on the side of the building, a rapid halt at the corner of the second left, he sees now Henry Road, tree-lined, suburban north London, and he watches as she… where is she? There. Walking up to a new-build, modern block, house? Apartments? Two lions, mews cobbles, she's in the door of, he sees now, the… steps, and accessibility ramp, angular, modernist, honey brick. A red sign below, 'St Thomas More Catholic Church, Manor House, Diocese of…'

Paul takes a breath, takes in his surroundings. No windows to the front. What chances in the cobbled paths to left and right of the building? You can see in his face the thought, what does she want with a church? That thing with the priest weeks back. She said Catholic upbringing. Has mentioned it a few times through the years. Never said she wasn't any more, just nothing about it at all. Only her least favourite thing, having to go to confession when she was ten, eleven, maybe. Then the things she pulled to get out of confession except for one last time until at fourteen she said she wasn't going to either it, confession, or mass, in fact, ever again. So long ago now I can't actually remember

117

what she said the reaction was. Just that she got her way. One time, maybe, she said that being brought up a Catholic was a good grounding for her stuff now, in her job, and the fire of indignation that drives everything they do, for the causes, the same rage but knowing what to do with it, and what to do with it is take action. Like a Liberation Theology thing? Or was it because she was being ironic, the strictures of a Catholic education all you need to know about kicking against the pricks endlessly and for ever? Can't remember now. Maybe a mix of them both. The indignation of what you are formed by being what you are against, and in the strongest possible terms. I said something once and she said, 'I wasn't ever abused by them, if that's what you're insinuating, not in so far as abused more than the subtle abuse of doctrinal brain washing.' So, now memory comes and she has been more than neutral. There. Through a window by the side of the building, he's in the mews to the left of the church and she's in confab with a priest. Sitting across from each other. A discussion? Or how they do confession these days? After he watches her leave and the priest come out and take the air he heads back out on to Henry Road, Alexandra Grove, Seven Sisters and away.

3.3

'I hear you have something for us,' the guv'nor says.

'Yes,' says Paul. 'I thought I was on pain of death if I didn't bring a real report to you this time.'

'You are,' says the guv'nor. There's a pause. 'I'm a busy man, Paul, and I don't mess about,' the guv'nor says.

'Yeah,' says Paul.

'Come on, then, out with it. Give your report, constable.'

'Four days ago. Two oh six PM. She visited the priest again. At his accommodation next to the church. I couldn't see what was happening in there, but then they left and went into the church proper. She was there for twenty-seven minutes in total, accommodation and church proper. She exited alone at two thirty-three PM. The priest came out five minutes later.'

'You stuck with the church, not the target?'

'I thought that would yield something... I mean, I know the target, know what she would look like on her return to the house. I know you'll say I should never *know* the target. Never assume, ass of you and me and all that. But I *know* this target. In this situation, at least. There's nothing she could do to surprise me.'

'Really?'

'Really. *Really* really. Give me that.'

The guv'nor slightly nods his head, a gesture of acceptance.

'*Really* really,' Paul says.

'OK. Speculation.'

'She's talking to him about... um... her marriage. Her relationships with her kids. The next day she started baking cupcakes...'

'Cup *what*?'

'Cupcakes. Little cakes. Little one-mouthful type cakes.'

'Aw, fairy cakes?'

'What?'

'It's what my mother called them.'

'Really? Huh.'

'OK. Speculation.'

'A bake sale, for the church? I mean, the cakes never hit our table. I think she said they were for a thing at her work, someone's birthday. But I know she never took them to her work. She was out four times in total this week when I didn't have eyes on her. I mean, when she was elsewhere than at her work.'

'So she could also have been back round at the church during her work time?'

'Could have.'

'OK,' the guv'nor says. 'I don't like it.'

'Maybe she has just got religion. Or her religion back.'

'Hmm. Could be. Could be not. Could be.'

'Why not?'

'Just. You have eyes on someone for twenty years and then something you weren't expecting comes up. That's when I feel uneasy. My liver starts hurting. I don't like it. What kind of cakes did you say they were again?'

'Cupcakes.'

'Anything else?'

'Not that I saw.'

'No cookies or brownies or anything?'

'Not that I… What do the details of *this* matter?'

'What have I told you a million times? When the overall picture won't come clear, run the details through, then again, then again. Until they fucking come clear.'

'Yeah, but cakes?'

The guv'nor bites at his thumbnail on his right hand. Doesn't quite bite. Gnaws. Sort of gnaws. Put it down as, *The guv'nor gnaws at his thumbnail.* Right-hand detail unimportant. 'So, what do you think?' the guv'nor says.

'It's the going in to the church bit that keeps me up nights.'

'Go on.'

'Well, the church she's back at, priests, Catholics, am I right?'

'Right.'

'Right. And they still have confession, don't they?'

'Well, I think loads of places still have confession, guv'nor.'

'Aye, but the Catholics, they're known for it, am I correct?'

'Maybe so.'

'So, a Catholic, back to her old ways, going to church with a priest and all that. Meets him in the accommodation, but they have to go next door into the actual place, the church. Why? What's in there they need?'

'You think she's confessing to him?'

'What do you think? That's happening. Question is, what's she confessing to him *about*?'

'Told you. Her crappy marriage, no doubt. Her useless husband. Isn't that what there is for a woman married twenty-five years?'

'You'd know.'

'Not sure I would.'

'You might be right.'

'What you reckon your wife would say about you?'

'I… see what you're saying.'

'Anything else?'

'Only the priest thing seems out of the ordinary.'

'And the cakes,' says the guv'nor.

'The cakes.'

'These… *cup*cakes. Nothing else?'

'She did say she was visiting the Oval in the near future.'

'The oval what?'

'The cricket ground. You know.'

'OK. We'll get that checked out. We must have a cricket fan in here somewhere.'

'Somewhere.'

'I'm just thinking, the Oval, is it actually an oval?'

'Oval?'

'Aye, is the place an oval? Is it ovular?'

'Ovular?'

'Aye, you know, ovular. The shape of it.'

'I don't think ovular is a word.'

'Eh?'

'You just say, is it oval? Is this circular thing an oval?'

'Circular can be oval?'

'Well, you know what I mean. Round thing. Is this round thing oval, an oval?'

'Not ovular?'

'If that is a word, probably has something to do with women, women's, you know. Ovulation and stuff.'

'Naw. I don't think so. Ovular. Oval. Ovular. So, we need a cricketer or cricket fan and a woman on this. I'll get back to you.'

'Don't we need a Catholic and a baker to swell the ranks?'

'Don't get funny. It's not funny. You aren't funny.'

'Never mean to be.'

'Naw. Right. Anyway, it's definitely the church, priest, Catholic, confession thing. That is fucking me off now.'

'I thought so.'

Wait. This has become a bit confusing. Can we replay that bit? But name who's who?

'She did say she was visiting the Oval in the near future.' Right, so that's definitely Paul.

'The oval what?' So that's the guv'nor.

'The cricket ground. You know.' Paul again.

'OK. We'll get that checked out. We must have a cricket fan in here somewhere.' The guv'nor.

'Somewhere.' That's Paul.

'I'm just thinking, the Oval, is it actually an oval?' The guv.

'Oval?' Paul.

'Aye, is the place an oval? Is it ovular?' Guv.

'Ovular?' Paul.

'Aye, you know, ovular. The shape of it.' Guv.

'I don't think ovular is a word.' Paul.

'Eh?' Guv.

'You just say, is it oval? Is this circular thing an oval?' Paul.

'Circular can be oval?' Guv.

'Well, you know what I mean. Round thing. Is this round thing oval, an oval?' Paul.

'Not ovular?' The guv'nor.

'If that is a word, probably has something to do with women, women's, you know. Ovulation and stuff.' Back to Paul.

'Naw. I don't think so. Ovular. Oval. Ovular. So, we need a cricketer or cricket fan and a woman on this. I'll get back to you.' The guv.

'Don't we need a Catholic and a baker to swell the ranks?' That's Paul.

'Don't get funny. It's not funny. You aren't funny.' The guv.

'Never mean to be.' Paul.

'Naw. Right. Anyway, it's definitely the church, priest, Catholic, confession thing. That is fucking me off now.' Guv.

'I thought so.' Paul.

'Aye. OK. Something to get going on, eh, Paul? How do you think this all relates to the, you know, protester stuff?'

'Still working on that, guv.'

'Aye?'

'Some of them are religious, but not many. Don't know how that Venn works. Some overlap. Something.'

'Work on that aspect. OK.' The guv'nor stares at Paul for a moment. 'Well?' the guv'nor says. 'Dismissed.'

3.4

A month later Julia is baking up a storm in the kitchen, focaccias for a fundraiser, she says. It doesn't sound right to him. Sure, there were things they were involved in for the causes which the other was not involved in much, but usually that was because he'd be involved in one aspect and she'd be involved in another. But, now, well, he's an outed rozzer, old bill, so no one's going to be involving him much, are they? So she says. She doesn't know about the people who have been getting in touch with him – he hasn't told her yet. Maybe never will. Lots of different reasons. One looking for money to become an informant, a nice little piece of knowledge to back-pocket; another wanting to tell him that they know he is for real in the organisation, because the twenty, twenty-five years, who couldn't have come round to the true cause, the true causes, in all that time: sheer logic prevails. And all points in between these two poles.

When she heads out on a Saturday mid-morning with two trays holding four large square focaccias for slicing up he waits the required amount of time then follows her. When she turns into Seven Sisters he feels he knows where she's going and takes a different route towards the Thomas More. As he gets to the corner with the best viewing angle, Portland Rise and Henry Road, sure enough, the bunting's up and the trestle tables are covered with paper tablecloth rolls. There are people milling about, a small gathering of them around the priest, others buying all sorts, some buying focaccia, Julia selling it and placing the pound coins in a plastic box. It takes about an hour for him to conclude that what is actually going on right in front of his eyes is exactly just what it is.

Next, the same evasive actions from Paul in getting there, you know, the trail of cameras tracing his route across London, and we're in Scotland Yard again with the guv'nor. 'So what was she doing there again?' the guv'nor says.

'Fundraising,' Paul says.

'For the church? Not one of the causes?'

'The church,' says Paul. 'Well. Looked like it.'

'She told you this, this time?'

'She said she was doing a fundraiser. I mean, over the years she's done a million of them. She didn't say what it was for.'

'And that's unusual?'

'No,' Paul says.

'So she has got religion, has she?'

'She always had one – she was brought up Catholic. Like I said, I'm sure that will be in the notes from way back.'

'You haven't reported on it recently?'

'You'd remember if I had. Right?'

'Of course. Mibby. Naw. I remember big picture, not details. Remind me. Religion.'

'Hasn't come up in years. Not until all this started.'

'So, she's gone back to her religion. And she's fundraising, eh?' says the guv'nor. From the look on his face he's calculating something, thinking something through. 'Harmless?' he says.

'Think so. I mean, I don't—'

'Mm. OK. I don't like it. I don't like when people change. I like it when they stay the same. Same is better. What's the name of the church again?'

'Thomas More Catholic Church. Up in Finsbury, off—'

'Aye. I don't like that in particular.'

'Oh?' says Paul.

'Thomas More? Not at all.'

'What, Catholics?'

'Naw. Thomas More,' says the guv'nor.

'What's so wrong with Thomas More?'

'What? He opposed his king. Traitor, really. Can't trust them.'

'Catholics?'

'Traitors.'

'You seem unusually knowledgeable about Thomas More,' Paul says.

'*The Man For All Seasons*? I loved that film. Phillip Schofield. And I've been reading those books by that lady, you know, um… Mantel.'

'Mantel?'

'You know the lady, Hilary Mantel. She's all over the shop. The Booker lady. Few years back.'

'Paul. And he's dead.'

'What? One of your new tricks, is it? Mystifying messages?'

'No, I'm just saying, the actor—'

'Anyway, books about Henry the Eighth and all that. Thomas More. Traitor. Wrote the book *Utopia*, envisioned it as a police state, really. Fucking spies everywhere, you know?'

'Thomas More?'

'Aye. All that. So. She goes up there much?'

'Took me a little while to figure it all out and piece it together, but she's also been disappearing some Saturday early evenings and some early Sunday mornings.'

'And you don't know or ask her where she's off to?'

'We've been together a long, long time for that stuff. She could be just off out to the shops, you know, to buy flowers or gloves or something like that, or out for a coffee. And since she knows I'm a copper, well… I mean. Do you always know where your wife is?'

'Absolutely, aye! I do, actually. What if she has an accident or something?'

'Really? I have just had to let her get on with stuff like that, even if it compromised the operation. I mean, I disappear so often myself. There's only so many excuses.'

'And you're saying she was fundraising?'

'Yeah.'

'Doing the cake stall again?' says the guv'nor.

'Focaccia, but yeah.'

'Focaccia? What's that? A cake?'

'An Italian bread, a spongy bread kind of thing.'

'Spongy?'

'Kind of like that. You make it with potato.'

'Ho! Wait a fucking minute, here. Spongy potato bread? What the fuck? You north London gits. Fuck me.'

'It's Italian.'

'Fucking better be, pal. Fucking bread potato sponge. Jesus.'

'So, I suppose that was what she was discussing with him a couple of weeks back.'

'Who?'

'The priest,' Paul says.

'The fucking Italian potato bread sponge?'

'The fundraising.'

'Aye… I suppose.'

'Unless she was getting confession.'

'Confessing? Confessing what?'

'Well, you know. Catholics. Confessing their sins and that.'

'What's this?'

'We've already been through this. It's a well known thing. You know. Church. Confession. Go to church. Confess your sins.'

'Don't get smart with me, fuckwit. I know what you're fucking talking about. That's no what's bothering me. What I mean is, what's she got to confess about? You think she was confessing? You saw this?'

'I didn't stay on after I'd established her location and activity that time. Didn't seem a point.'

The guv'nor is staring at Paul.

'I saw them talking, her and the priest. Didn't see anything that looked like confession. Can't see what it can matter if she's just got a wee yen on her for her religion and she's telling the priest all the mean things she thinks about this and that. She hasn't been murdering anyone... as far as I know. She doesn't lie and cheat and go out on the rob.'

'I do not like this,' the guv'nor says.

'What's the big deal? That's the conclusion I'm coming to, anyway. She's barely active with ORGAN:EYES, even, these days.'

'Confessing. Telling all. Fucking whisper, whisper, whisper, it was like this, father, whisper, whisper, whisper, it was like that, father. Fuck. She could be telling him anything. Anything.'

'Telling him anything what? I can't see—'

'You can't see?'

'Well. I mean. Am I missing something here?'

'I just don't fucking like it, is all.'

The sarge walks in. He's wearing a sort of... safari suit?

'Christ. I'm tired,' Paul says. 'I think I am off my game. Missing something. Feel like me missing something is leading to us all missing something.'

'You've been through a lot recently, sonny boy,' the sarge says.

'Yeah?' says Paul.

'Aye, well, that slight fuck-up with the mental ward thing,' the sarge says.

The guv'nor turns to the sarge, staring, and the sarge turns to the guv. Then they both look back at Paul, smiling. Baring their teeth, at least.

'Ah, I was as well-off in there as anywhere. Almost straight off I thought it was probably preferable to being back at the old man and old lady's, anyway. Jesus, what would I have to say to them, these days? At least on the wards there were some nice nutters to talk to. The A-MEE-rican guy. He was OK.'

'Mibby it is some time with your parents you need.'

'What?'

'Just saying. Mibby you need a wee reconnect to who you are?'

'Who I am? Jesus. That guy died years ago, I think. Who I am. Christ.'

'OK. Guess you're right.'

'Do you even want to be who you were twenty or thirty years back?'

'See what you're saying?'

'Yeah.'

'Something bothering you, Paul? You can tell old Uncle Sarge if you like.'

'Jesus,' Paul says. 'My wife thought – and probably still thinks – I make jokes about Madeleine McCann.' He takes a deep breath. 'It's the stuff around the stuff that can be almost worse. Like that other case. A wee girl is abducted, raped and murdered and the crazies and freaks come out. Not from the woodwork, more from the slime that forms on the wood. She's killed and one crazy sends letters making death threats to her sister and tells the sister that he killed the wee girl. Another freak phones up the family pretending to be their wee girl. Another crazy emails the family, the police and family friends saying the murder is a cover-up, that really the girl has been trafficked out to Romania to work as a stripper and prostitute. Christ. And the whole time the police are investigating the father, and when the trial for the actual abductor, rapist, murderer finally gets going the family are put through the wringer while the shit sits it out mostly. And is it any less crazy that the family had been led to believe their little girl was still alive because her phone was buzzing with usage that was actually the papers hacking, tampering and generally dickying with the messages and texts?'

'We don't live in a perfect world, Paul.'

'No we don't,' Paul says, 'A sweet pea was named after the other wee girl, in memoriam. A sweet pea? The nut investigator who uses some sort of box that means satellites and DNA can find the wee one, the fucked-up faith that makes anyone think the Pope can intercede, the fucked-up faith of the Pope who thinks prayer can produce miracles. And, come on, fine enough when the coke-head sniffer dogs go apeshit for their next hit, but really Lassie is not going to save the day. All the freaks and crazies who say they know exactly what happened, they just aren't being listened to. The frauds who collect money for the wee one's fund, the demented demanders of two million euros for information related to, the crazy false claimers, hoaxers, hoax-claimers. And the hollow, callow, despicable user politicians, police officers, journalists doing fuck all but evil or fuck all at all. How I burn incandescent for the girl, the wee one, the girls, all the wee ones, from the knowing, the not knowing, the never knowing.' He looks around himself. 'I mean,' he says, 'what I mean,' he says, 'is, really, only a cynic would exploit this story.'

'Are you OK, Paul?' the guv'nor says.

'Ah, probably the melon twister of being on the wards. Probably. You know the hardest bit? I couldn't stand being away from my daughters. My... daughters... I just couldn't...'

'We know, pal. We get it. These things are never easy.'

'*Never easy?* Jesus, that's the understatement of the fucking year.'

The guv'nor stands up and says, 'Look, fuckwit, we all know what fucked up here. We sent you in and none of us really knew about the state of your marriage, did we? We're not all fucking Mystic Meg. OK. Fucking annoying. Not the end of the world. Christ, it was as good as sending you in if you'd been single, but these things happen.'

'The future came up and bit me, yeah. Bit us all. Christ!'

'Listen, Paul, you do need some time somewhere grounded. Go spend time with your daughters.'

'Yeah,' Paul says, collecting his things and getting ready to leave.

'Thanks, Paul, but I got to get on. I'm a busy man and I don't mess about,' the guv'nor says.

'Yeah?' Paul says, turning at the door, breaking. 'Doing what?'

'Take it easy, Paul,' the guv'nor says.

3.5

After Paul leaves, the guv'nor walks along with the sarge to his office.

'Has he got anything?' the sarge says. 'Does he know what's going on?'

'I'm no sure,' says the guv'nor. 'He's starting to wonder. I don't like that. Reporting. I like reporting. I don't like wondering. Fucking prick.'

The sarge says, 'Don't know he's got much more in his bag of tricks.'

'Bag of tricks?' says the guv'nor. 'It's "box of tricks". What are you saying? Bag of tricks?'

'Bag of tricks, box of tricks. Same thing.'

'It's box of tricks. Box? Box,' the guv'nor says, distractedly.

The sarge says nothing, half-turns, preparing to leave, only waiting to hear whether he'll be dismissed. As he quarter-turns further the guv'nor says, 'Oh. Get this focaccia thing checked out. I want to know everything.'

'You want to know where you can get some focaccia?' says the sarge. 'Sure. I'll find out.'

'No that. Jesus Christ. Hendon fuckwit. I want to know about anything going on that might be signalled by focaccia. Any codes being used out and about.'

'Focaccia. Right. Got it. Like the men who were Sunday, Monday, Thursday thing, eh? It's an Italian bread, hin't it? Made with potatoes.'

'I fucking know that bit already! Fucking God.'

The guv'nor sits down at the table again, sighs and wipes across his forehead with his hand.

'Problem, guv?' says the sarge.

'I don't know,' says the guv'nor. 'This is getting a bit messy.'

'Getting?' says the sarge.

The guv'nor looks up at the sarge, fierce looking, then he softens. 'Aye, OK. Point taken.'

'Anything I should be doing?'

'Let me think.'

'Take your time, guv. I don't think there's anything that should be done – nothing hasty, put it that way.'

'No. No. Christ, if there's any case that proves you have to play the long game. But I'll tell you this, it will not end in a long mess. I'm not having that. All the Noseys getting in on it and that.'

'Sound a bit like Paul is going to disappear off the face of the earth one fine day, guv.' The sarge makes a magician's *foof* gesture. 'Just like that.'

'Naw, come on. You know that doesnae happen.'

'Any more,' the sarge says and smiles.

The guv'nor smiles and shakes his head.

'Christ, sometimes I look at these blank walls, blank ceilings, blank fucking table, even, and I just feel—'

'Blank?'

The guv'nor gives another fierce look, one that doesn't subside as quickly.

The sarge shrugs and rolls his shoulders, clears his throat and, 'Had to,' he says.

'I feel, if you'll let me finish, what are we doing, what am I doing, spending my life in fucking blank rooms like this? Paul's right, "Doing what?" Doing what.'

'Aye,' says the sarge. 'It is a bit Samuel Beckett.'

'Who?' the guv'nor says.

'Irish. Wrote bleak plays. Funny, though.'

'The fucking things you come out with, sarge.'

'Have to read for the job, know things the scrotes know.'

'Aye, I suppose. Christ, even the faces look blank to me now.'

'Aye. Nothing faces. No faces at all.'

'Aye. Anyway, this Paul sitch, I do not know. I just do not know. What do you make of him?'

'Paul?'

'Aye.'

'He's been a good boy over the years – got himself way in over the maximum head height, sure, but, you know, brought home the bacon on several occasions, tasty bacon. Of course, the, um, domestic arrangements are not ideal, a bit fucked up if I'm being honest with you, but then whose hin't?'

'Mm. I see what you're saying. Aye. I thought we were the bacon, though.'

'I'm no pig.'

'We're all pigs.'

'So, how do we resolve this? I guess is what we have to ask ourselves.' … 'Guv? Is that what we have to ask ourselves?' says the sarge.

'Aye, it is,' the guv'nor says.

'So. Is there anything I should be doing right now?'

The guv'nor sits for a while staring at the blank table, blank walls, glancing at the blank ceiling a couple of times. He pulls some fluff off his cuff, lets it fall to the blank floor.

'Harold Pinter, now,' says the sarge.

'Who?'

'Another playwright.'

'Aye?'

'Aye.'

'Irish too?'

Pause.

'Naw.'

Finally, the guv'nor says, 'Give it some time and then we're sacking him for gross misconduct.'

'Misconduct?' the sarge says, genuinely surprised.

'He fucked the target, for fuck's sake,' the guv'nor says. 'Had kids with her. Aye, misconduct. Aye, gross. False representation, is it not?'

'But we told him—'

'He didn't tell us about the state of his fucking relationship when he went in.'

'Well, no.'

'Well, no. Well, no. That's what I'm saying.'

'OK. Soon? Months?'

'Naw. I want some brownie points with some Interpol stuff. I want him over with the Johnny Foreigners. I want him on some dirty ops.'

'When, then?' the sarge says.

'Couple of years,' the guv'nor says. 'Right. Take it easy.'

The sarge turns and walks out of the blank room, and the guv'nor hears, 'Well, well, now. The plot thickens!'

3.6

To clear his head, Paul takes a walk around his local park in the evening. There's been a lot of it, recently, if you know what he means. He just needs his head to clear. He hears his name being said, close by, not loud, and the two of them are right at his back as he turns. He looks down at their shoes, because whatever they're wearing, he needs a pair, able to get that close up behind him without him noticing.

'All right, lads,' Paul says. They must be in their twenties. 'What way's this going, then?'

'Not that way, not the other way,' says the tallest lad.

'OK,' Paul says. 'I'll stop clenching, shall I?'

'You'd be on safe ground, mate,' the taller one says.

'Do I get names?' Paul says.

'Call me A,' says the shorter one.

'That'll make you B, will it?' Paul says.

'Sure, why no?' says B.

'You lads both from Scotland?'

'How?' says B.

'Just a theory I've got on the go.'

'Aye, though he's a sheepshagger from Aberdeen. That doesnae count as decent Scottish. They're aw Vikings and Picts, urn't they?' says B.

'And you're from Berwick. That's practically English, yuh fuck,' says A.

'Is that why the A and B?'

'How?' says B.

'Aberdeen and Berwick?'

They look at each other and then turn to Paul, both at the same time saying, 'Naw.'

'Stupendous,' Paul says. 'Let me run my theory a wee bit longer. The Met, right?'

'Well, aye. Sort of,' says A. 'MIB.'

'Oh, the men in black, is it? Now I see the letter naming thing.'

'You know what MIB is,' says B. 'Metropolitan Investi—'

'Calm down, lads. Of course I do. Let's cut to the chase, shall we? What do you young Turks at the Metropolitan Investigations Bureau want with an old codger like me?'

'Well, Paul, right now you're about as famous as a copper gets.'

'It's a privilege to perform,' Paul says.

'You've been, what, a hundred years dug in on the other side?' Paul shrugs.

'And now you're shown up as the big betrayer of all the leftie loonies,' says A.

134

Paul shrugs again.

'You've been called all sorts in the papers and stuff, but basically what every leftie thinks is that you're a cunt, plain and simple.'

'Yeah, thanks for that, lads.'

'We like that. For the purposes of what we're working on, you see.'

'Oh yeah?' Paul says. 'And what's that?'

'Far right.'

'Inside the inside of the Met? You mean you're working on making us the far right?'

'Aye, funny.'

'OK, where do I fit in?'

'Biggest cunt for the lefties? We were thinking, head of a far-right movement? Fancy it?'

'Me? You want me for that gig?'

'Naw, we actually want Tommy Robinson, but he's too young just yet.'

Paul heaves a laugh, a sigh, snorts. 'Sorry, I've got other things cooking,' he says. A and B are looking at Paul. Three men standing silently in the evening in the park. 'So, anyway,' Paul says, 'show me your skills.' He turns to face where he was walking before this conversation began, turns back and A and B are gone, disappeared like a magic trick.

The next evening, the Tuesday, bin night, Julia is putting a bin out, walking the first bin along the side and out to the front of the house. Paul is at the back door, just about to walk the second bin out when Julia rushes back round the side of the house. 'Jesus! Someone's breaking into the bloody car!' she calls out.

'You are kidding me,' Paul says.

'He's just about to smash the—!' Julia calls.

There's a smashing sound that they both hear. Paul is off like a jackrabbit, through the house, pulling the front door open, out the front door and after this man with a towel around his arm and a metal bolster in his hand by the look of it. Julia comes round the side of the house and Paul catches sight of her as he glances back. 'He could have a weapon!' Julia is calling behind Paul. Maybe she hasn't seen the bolster, or doesn't think it makes enough of a weapon itself.

The would-be car thief startles. He starts running, but first his arm seems stuck in the hole in the driver side window and then he isn't fast. Probably drugs as well as the booze you could smell on him, even from where we are here. He stumbles.

'Wanker!' Paul is shouting. 'Fucking... STOP!'

As he gets to him, Paul gives him a shove as opposed to the grab the thief's so obviously waiting for, loosening his jacket and trying to take it off. He goes down, no problem at all, splayed out like a starfish. But it's this that causes Paul, at full pelt, to trip over and away from the man and end up on the ground just past the man's head. Paul's still on the ground as he watches the man get up and start running again, off in a different direction. And it's from the ground that you can see him watch as Julia, his wife, the mother of his kids, come tearing up and get a foot in front of the man's right calf, a move that would make a defender proud. A dirty-playing defender. Paul is up and heading for two heaps on the ground, loosening his arms ready to put a hold on the man.

That's when he pauses as he watches Julia shout out, 'FUCKER!' and launch her body from her position to land on the man, grab at his right arm and twist it behind him and up his back. By the time Paul gets to them, Julia has the man upright and in some pain the way she's holding his arm. Paul is looking at his wife, and she glances around at him. Her hold slackens and he takes the man's arm, goosenecks his wrist and secures his stance, places his left hand as per regulations on the man's left shoulder and braces.

The man says, 'Fuck's sake, if I'd known you two knew control and restraint, I wouldn't have fucking bothered with your fucking car, would I?'

Paul is looking at Julia, patently puzzled. 'I just… when you… ran…' Then, breathless, he smiles.

3.7

The door to the pub opens and closes behind Julia, and she sees the young woman sitting over in a corner, nursing a glass of white wine.

'Hello Julia,' Natasha says.

'Yeah, hi,' Julia says. 'How are things with you?'

'Oh, you know. Still trying to get my story… I mean, your story, up and running. It's taking longer than I hoped.'

'Yeah? That's maybe no bad thing. You wouldn't want to get it wrong, would you? You might get in a lot of trouble and end up a laughing stock, yeah?'

'I don't know why, but that sounds like a sort of threat, you know?'

'I don't make threats. I was talking about other people.'

'Mmm. Do you want to talk about the money?'

'Talk about it? No, I don't want to talk about it. I just want to receive it, if that's OK?'

'You know what I mean − if we're meeting again then we probably have to negotiate a new amount, am I correct?'

'Yes, there'll be a new amount every time there's a new conversation. You know that's understood.'

'I do now. Thanks for the clarification.'

'There's no point getting sarky with me. You want the story, so you pay. There's a price in all these things.'

'Yes, there is. Seems to me you've paid the highest price of us all.'

'How do you figure that?'

'Come on, Julia.'

'No, you come on, say what you have to say.'

'Well, you've had your life stolen from you. You're the one who's been tricked.'

'What life's that, then?'

'*Your* life. The life you could have had if Paul hadn't come along and fucked… everything up.' Natasha smiles. 'Your real life. The person you really should have married, the kids you really should have had.'

'My kids? Really? I'd prefer, actually, that as we get into our… transaction, you keep your nose out of my life, whether you think of it as real or not.'

'I don't know how that's going to work.'

'Oh, it'll work. I'll make it work. I'll make sure it works. And you'll be keeping my kids out of it.'

'But that is the story, Julia.'

'No. Paul is the story. Concentrate on him. I told you where to find him, by the way, so you could go and have a look at him, not so you could wade in all guns blazing.'

'I didn't. But he wouldn't stop staring at me. I thought it would look weird if I didn't acknowledge that, if only to tell him to bugger off and leave me alone.'

'That's not what I'm hearing.'

'Oh, Julia. Don't you get it? He'll tell you anything he wants you to hear. Haven't you learned anything yet?'

'Fuck off. You really think you know what's going on, don't you?'

'No, I want *you* to tell me what's really going on.'

'Yeah, well leave my kids out of it. They're off limits.'

'But that is the story, Julia. The story of state rape—'

'Woah! Stop.'

Julia sits thinking for a while. She wishes she had bought a drink before sitting down. Then she says, 'Your name is Natasha Whately-Smith-Michael, yeah? Isn't it?'

'So?'

'Little rich girl, is it?'

'That's a bit of a stereotype.'

'I'm right, though, aren't I? From up north, but posh north, aren't you?'

'If that's what you think.'

'Yeah, it is. Durham, eh? Nice little village, maybe. Or is it Daddy's nice big farm? The country estate? Yeah, you smell a bit of the farm.'

Natasha says nothing.

'Three fucking surnames. Jesus.'

Natasha says nothing.

'No? No comment, eh?'

Natasha says nothing.

'Nothing to say. Interesting. Because I'm right. Daddy's nice big farm and estate. Big tussle over the land, eh? Though you could be just shopkeeper class, really.'

Natasha says nothing.

'Because it's really the collapse of marriage and feminism doing for patronymic names and bringing matronymic naming into popularity. All over around here, getting close to there being no kids with single surnames in Islington. Let's look at some basic facts, shall we? A double surname is heritable, and mostly taken in order to preserve a family name that would have become extinct due to the absence of male descendants bearing the name, connected to the inheritance of a family estate.'

'If you say so.'

'Yeah, I do. These indicate prima facie the inheritance of multiple estates and thus the consolidation of great wealth. These are sometimes created when the legator has a double-barrelled name and the legatee has a single surname, or vice versa. Nowadays, these names are almost always abbreviated in everyday usage to a single or double-barrelled version. So, you get it? It's about class and aristocracy and keeping the money because there was money to tussle over. Then you get more money in the middle classes after Victorian times, more second marriages for all classes after the wars because of dead husbands and then more divorces into the nineteen sixties and even more second marriages. I mean, this is when it really starts to fall apart, and then everyone is trying to cling on to the money and then ideological feminism comes in and 'Victimisation Position Number One', marriage, and marriage getting dumped. So, all that taking a man's name? I mean, think of the introduction of a woman using the old style – she actually took it all, and it was Mrs David Smith, Mrs Victor Killermont. Etiquette is etiquette. I kid you not. So, fuck that, say wimmin in the seventies, I'm keeping my own name, first professionally, then just everywhere and then you get to 'We're both getting our surnames on the kids' certificates.'

Natasha raises an eyebrow.

'But the thing is, if you're doing that, you need some sort of *system*. Like in Spain, a person will take the first surname of the father, followed by the first surname of the mother, their maternal grandfather's surname. A system, see? OK, *but*, surnames are strictly regulated by the Civil Code and the Law of the Civil Registry. When a person is born, the law requires them to take the first surname of the father and then the first surname of the mother. In Germany double surnames can be taken upon marriage, written with or without hyphen, combining the husband's surname with the wife's or the other way chronologically, *Allianznamen*, rather than *Doppelnamen*. There is the possibility that one partner can combine both names by a hyphen. So, one of them then bears a double name, *Doppelname*, so like Herr Braun and Frau Meyer-Braun or Frau Braun-Meyer; but, get this, the children have to be called Braun. Only one partner can take this option, making it impossible for both partners to have *Doppelnamen*. There would be no Herr Meyer-Braun and Frau Meyer-Braun. And, a 1993 law forbids surnames with more than two components. There has to be some kind of limiting, you see.'

'If you say so.'

'Or, in Switzerland, the first name is the official family name, which will be inherited by the legitimate children. So, when Werner Stauffacher marries Gertrud Baumgarten, both can use the name Stauffacher-Baumgarten. Their children Heinrich and Verena, however, bear only the surname Stauffacher. See, rules. Need rules. Lately, based on feminist pressure, wives have been permitted by law to place their original birth name before the family name. This double name is written without a hyphen and is borne by the wife only. So, it's Gertrud Baumgarten Stauffacher, while her husband's name is Werner Stauffacher and the children's names remain, say, Heinrich and Verena Stauffacher. And you just know the kind of tortuous referenda that would have led to this Swiss setting of rules. Going over to Russia and a Federal law, for fuck's sake, number 143-FZ 'On Civil State Acts' explicitly allows double-barrelled names in Article 28, but limits such compound surnames to two parts only.'

'You seem well versed in all this. It's a particular interest of yours?'

'If *you* say so. I mean, often the whole thing is necessary as a response to some other stupidity in the population. The overwhelming preponderance in Wales of only a few surnames such as Jones, Williams and Davies led to the usage of double-barrelled names in order to just avoid confusion of unrelated but similarly-named people. I mean, sort it out some other way, people.'

Natasha blinks.

'Anyway, the Islington problem, and probably London and probably the whole country is, there're no rules once you've slid into a double-barrel free-for-all. Let's give the example at its most exponential, shall we? Alexandra Bates and Bailey Fitzsimmons get together and have two children, Ben and Belinda Bates-Fitzsimmons, while Caitlin Sim gets together with Charlie Broomfield to have one child, Marianne Sim-Broomfield. Ben and Marianne get together and have four children: Joshua, Danielle, Daisy and Edward Bates-Fitzsimmons-Sim-Broomfield. Then Daisy and Elena Proudfoot-Akinsanya-Adeluka-Racova have a child, Ellis Bates-Fitzsimmons-Sim-Broomfield-Proudfoot-Akinsanya-um-Adeluka-Racova, who gets together with Heather Mewse-Blanco-Doctrove-Joseph-whatever-Wright-Benford-Green-Eliasson and have two children: Henry and Jade Bates-Fitzsimmons-Sim-Broomfield-Proudfoot-Akinsanya-Adeluka-Racova-um-um-Mewse-Blanco-Doctrove-um-Joseph-Wright-Benford-Green-Eliasson. Jade gets together with James Foulger-Vasile-eh-Viezure-Holmes-Lenton-Wilson-um-Chambers-Khakoo-Leppard-eh-Bridgland-Kleanthous-Lenanton-Dean-Wells-Fowler-Philpot and have two children: Jessica and Tobias Bates-Fitzsimmons-Sim-um-Broomfield-Proudfoot-Akinsanya-Adeluka-eh-Racova-Mewse-Blanco-Doctrove-Joseph-Wright-um-um-Benford-Green-Eliasson. Jack gets together with Tobias Foulger-Vasile-Viezure-Holmes-Lenton-Wilson-Chambers-Khakoo-Leppard-Bridgland-Kleanthous-Lenanton-Dean-Wells-Fowler-Philpot. Well, we can see a problem here. We've got Bates-Fitzsimmons-Sim-eh-eh-Broomfield-Proudfoot-Akinsanya-Adeluka-Racova-Mewse-Blanco-um-Doctrove-Wright-Joseph-Benford-Green-Eliasson-Foulger-Vasile-Viezure-Holmes-Lenton-Wilson-Chambers-Khakoo-Leppard-Bridgland-Kleanthous-Lenanton-Dean-Wells-Fowler-fucking-Philpot kids on our hands! If you don't see the problem you're as stupid as you look.' Julia is about out of breath.

'Wow. That's quite a performance,' Natasha says.

'Do you have any fucking idea, any fucking idea at all, how intelligent I have to be to do the job I do? For the people I do it for? Have you any fucking idea?' Julia says, jabbing her finger into the journalist.

'Don't think you can weirdly intimidate me by reeling off names like a stupid party trick.'

'Yeah?'

'I'm from the north. I don't intimidate easily.'

'You mean you don't *get intimidated* easily. Call yourself a fucking writer?'

'OK, just keep digging. Jog on.'

'From the north, eh, are you? Do you know what that pride in coming from the north means? It means you can't see there's a whole chunk of England which lies north of whatever shithole you come from, and north of that a whole other country. Scotland is granite, by the way; England is sandstone. One of these days we're getting washed away and all there'll be is Scotland. If anything, in Britain, just now, you're from a sort of middle of the main island. And you don't mean you come from north of anything but what lies south of you. All you can do, and you hate this, is compare yourself and stare at London. And you hate London. You hate their arrogance, the admiration of London by Londoners. Isn't that right? Except you give them that, coming from up north, as in north of *London only*. Because you're not thinking of north in terms of Europe, say, are you? How could that be? Because London is one of the northern European cities, a northern European capital city, isn't it? So you're not saying you're northern, north of Europe, because so are Londoners. Or maybe, stupidly, you do mean this. Is this what you mean? You're northern like all the other people in the northern hemisphere of the world, are you? No, you mean you're northern standing staring at London offering it all your doffed cloth cap obsequious bending over for the fuck up the arse from London. Northern. Spare me.'

Natasha is staring into her wine. 'You wanted… to talk about money, I think. Wasn't that it?'

'I'll give it some thought,' says Julia, 'I'll give it some thought,' as she stands and, 'Yeah, definitely going to give that some thinking time, all right,' as she walks out of the pub.

3.8

Next day Julia tells Paul that her work at the rape crisis charity is going to fill up her whole day. She takes the bus to Victoria Coach Station (cameras #5, #4, 2, 6, 3, BE, FE, SE, 6, 31, 22, 1, 3, 2, 1, FRONTGATE, 3, 8, 6, 23, 13, 1, 1, 5, 6, CB, AB), walks to the Tube and goes to Embankment, takes the Tube to Piccadilly Circus (cameras SE, S, SW, 32, 44, 6, 1, 4, No2, No3, No4, 3, 5, L, J, K, 3, 9, 7, 3, 2, X, XI, 4), then loses herself in the crowd for a while before going back to Embankment (cameras 7, 8, 6, 4, ftdr, f, #1, #7, #9, 6, 4, 12, Backgate, 25, 13, 5, Back, Side, Front, 7B, 5A, 27, 2, 5, 3, 4, 7, 4, 1, 5, B, A, 27, 6YG, 9, 6, 12, 14, 7, #3, 6, 4, 72, 8FD, 7BC, 9A, 13, 1, 42, 7B, 12, 2), then one stop along to Temple (cameras 17, 18, 19, 20, 4, 2, 1, 5, 4, 3, #3, #2). She leaves the Tube here and walks to Thames House (cameras 3, 5, 10, 9, 8, ██████████████████████), to an entrance she knows at the rear of the premises (cameras ██████████████████████████). After she pushes the buzzer and enters after a response (cameras ███████), she walks along a long corridor (cameras ███████), takes a lift up four floors (camera ███████), walks along another long corridor, around a corner (camera ███████), then a short corridor and into a small, anonymous room which has a window into the corridor but no window to the outside world. The boss is sitting across a table from her. She signals for Julia to sit in a cotton-upholstered chair in front of her. 'Hello Julia,' the boss says, 'How are you doing?'

'I'm OK, Suzie, how are you?' Julia says.

'It's been a busy time. How is Paul?'

'He's OK. A bit spooked by all the revelations, you know, little factettes popping up everywhere like rabbits pulled out of a hat.'

'I've got a joke for you on that one, remind me.'

'OK. Well, this Mark thing has got him riled as fuck.'

144

'Yeah? Poor man.'

'Oh yeah, poor man. Boo hoo.'

'Now, now, Julia. I've told you, you don't have to be like that when you're reporting to me. I'll allow anything in terms of your feelings about Paul. Jesus, I'd even accept you thinking of him as your actual loving husband. The fact he's the father of your kids is just incontrovertible.'

'I can live with that. He just pisses me off sometimes.'

'Yeah?'

'Suppose he's like all husbands in that sense.'

'Yeah.'

'And the stay in the hospital?'

'Who arranged that fuck-up?'

'I think that one got a little deranged more than arranged, to be honest. Word we're getting was he was supposed to spend some time with his ma and pa.'

'He hasn't seen them in years.'

'You sure?'

'Fairly. I don't bother checking on them specifically, but I do check where he goes when he's out of London, and he's never anywhere near where they live, that's for sure.'

'Yeah.'

'So where's he been recently?'

'Ha. Hackney, mostly. He says he's working at a new studio for that tinpot label of his.'

'And what's he really been doing over there?'

'Oh, he's got the hots for that journalist, you know the one.'

'She's a handful.'

'Yeah, I know.'

'Does it bother you?'

'No. He's harmless that way. Wouldn't know what to do with her if he did insinuate himself into her pants. He just likes watching, I think.'

'Is he dangerous to her, do you think?'

'Like I say. Harmless.'

'Maybe. Men can change.'

'We all can.'

'I suppose.'

'Did he come out of the loony bin different?'

'Subdued, mostly. They rammed him full of antipsychotics. He had played it by telling the truth, and of course they put him down as paranoid delusional, then as having a personality disorder. It took a while for his head to clear.'

'And now?'

'Back to boozing, but he has stayed on one of the drugs because he says when he stops he feels fucked.'

'Addicted?'

'If you want to call it that. I think, withdrawal symptoms, yeah.'

'And his thinking has changed?'

'Sort of. It's difficult, isn't it, when someone's mental. Are they acting the way they are because they're mental, or is it just one of their personality traits, exaggerated or whatever? I mean, personality disorder. We all know his personality is disordered. Being undercover has left him with no personality.'

'Or too many.'

'Yeah,' Julia says, and laughs. 'One too many. One more than he needs, yeah.'

'And him coming home?'

'It's fine,' Julia says. 'Much as we said it would go.'

'What's he said?'

'He confessed all. Just what you've read in the papers, really.'

'What about the money?'

'Nothing on that yet.'

'What have you told the girls?'

'We sat down with them. It was mostly about how we still love them, whoever we are. We, me and Paul, said we trusted each other. I kind of implied I always knew he was a copper. That kind of thing.'

'How did they take it?'

'I don't know. I think mostly they were pissed off they had been asked to turn their equipment off.'

'Equipment?'

'You have kids, don't you? Computer and TV, iPad. They're too young. What do they care about us and our nonsense?'

'So, he confessed all about who he is?'

'Think so. Nothing I didn't know already.'

'And did you – did you know?'

'What?'

'You know.'

'What?'

'Did you feel like doing a wee bit of confessing yourself?'

'What? No. You're kidding, right?'

'Well, you know, if it's cards-on-the-table time.'

'I just saw it as an opportunity. To get more out of him, you know.'

'Good. Good. You're keeping your head.'

'I always have.'

'Are you? Are you keeping your head?'

'Hey. Look. I'm twenty-odd years in on this. I've had kids by the wanker. Do you know what that takes?'

'OK.'

'Yeah?'

'OK. It's appreciated.'

'Yeah? Letting the fucker fuck me, get me up the duff? Twice. One way of looking at it is state rape, that little bitch Nosey said.'

'That's going it a bit, isn't it, Julia? I mean, some of the things I've done…'

'Yeah?'

'You always know it's appreciated.'

'Yeah, well, let me work. And just be ready to be there when I need you.'

'Meaning?'

'Yeah. All I give a bugger about, if and when the balloon goes up, is getting me and the kids out. Yeah? I want you to get me and the kids *out*.'

'You don't think this operation has legs any more?'

'Do you? Now?'

The boss shrugs.

'Hm. Yeah. It's fucked, mid and long term. What do you think the Met will do with him?'

'If I was his guv'nor I'd be planning a disappearance into Europe, some dirty ops. But he might be too dirty himself now for a disappearing act.'

A pause.

'You were going to tell me a joke.'

'Was I?'

'Something about rabbits and hats.'

'Oh yeah. Don't know I remember it now, but it's something about, "I can't pull a rabbit out of a hat, but I can pull a hare out of me arse."'

'Ha. Yeah, that's about the only trick we really know how to perform.'

'Yeah, the performance. Anyway, any particular destinations in mind for you?'

'Workwise?'

'If that's what's concerning you.'

'Five Eyes, I suppose. Signals intel. I hear good things about what the NSA are doing, and it could mean a move. Somewhere warm and sunny, even. For the girls.'

'OK. Right. Get back to work is all there is to say.'

Julia looks down herself sadly.

The boss says, 'Seriously, though, is he OK?'

'I will be serious, but you're not going to like it.'

'Just… go on.'

'Well, my answer to "Is he OK?" is, seriously, when have we ever cared, really? About him? He's just a triangulation, isn't he? We check our stuff against his and that's all there is to it. Sometimes I think he and me have been left to get on with it for all this time because... or rather *not* because we get such stunning information from him, but because we're both just such low-level, such bottom feeders in the whole circus, the last knife into the box for the magician's trick.'

'You think?'

'Yeah. To think anything else is just naïve.'

'I think maybe you're being naïve, Julia.'

'Oh?'

'It's possible. You are naïve in one way, at least, yeah.'

'Oh, now we're getting into it! Come on, then, out with it.'

'Haven't you worked it out yet, after all these years?'

'I'm sure you're about to tell me.'

'The information you've provided has been highly valuable. Invaluable, really. Priceless.'

'What, checks on checks on checks? What's so great about that?'

'You really don't get it, do you?'

'Really? Enlighten me. If I'm going to see, I want to see everything.'

'Oh, Julia, we've never been triangulating information with his information. We've never been working with the Met on this. What's been happening is... We've got to know what those Met fucks are up to.'

'I... Explain to me.'

'You went in to find out what the cunts were thinking they were doing, going in hard like that. They could have destabilised the whole country. I mean, fuck. Don't you see? We're the cunts who are watching what those fucking cunts think they're about.'

Julia comes out of Thames House at the back, walks over to the river and scratches at her stomach and rips the wire and microphone off, then she stops her phone recording. She takes a deep breath, then another. It doesn't help.

On Oxford Street, Julia watches herself enter H&M then River Island then John Lewis and Partners in CCTV monitors above her head as she enters, watches her back recede into the shops. All watching, a thousand per square mile, all over London and all over the world, people watching themselves walking into shops, around shops, down aisles, around corners. Or the cameras that people cannot see themselves on, people in Oxford Street. Clarks, H. Samuel, Niketown, Top Shop, Vans, Urban Outfitters, Schuh, Office, JD Sports, TK Maxx, Zara, Gap, Pandora, Ernest Jones, EE, Three, Foot Locker. People on camera, hundreds, thousands, tens of thousands, hundreds of thousands, millions upon millions of images of walking towards, turning away, turning towards, backs walking away, heads, shoulders, legs, a billion images of people up and down this street. Two women, one man, a woman with a baby in a buggy, a woman with three young children, two men, four men, two couples, a man, another man, another man, a woman, another woman, another man, another woman, two women with buggies apiece and a kid walking along in between them, a young person who might be a boy or a girl, a Mrs Baker, Ms Ballin, Mr Fletcher, Mr Adenuga, Ms Copeland, Mr Green, Mr Lodge, Ms O'Sullivan, Mr Lind, Ms Brown, Mrs Mews, Ms Tate, Mrs Woods, Mrs Wyatt, Ms Mensah, Mr Shanti-I, Ms Bailey, Mrs Richardson, Ms Bendeth, Mr Brown, Ms Bennett, Mr Colley, Ms Butler, Ms Deacon, Ms Conway, Mr Dean, Ms Abel, Mr Doherty, Ms Faith, Ms Shaw, Mr Harper, Mr Harrison, Ms Hennell, Mr Hill, Ms King, Mrs King, Mr King, Lord Lowe, Ms McCourt, Ms Samuels, Ms Lloyd, Mr MacDougal, Ms McLean, Mr Booker, Ms Agyeman, Mr Meyer, Mrs Moore, Ms Mwamwaya, Mr Nelson, Ms Macrae, Mrs Raworth, Mrs Schultz, Mrs Sirtis, Mr Reid, Smee, Ms Tandy, Mrs Whiteread, Ms Westerby, Mr Ritchie, Ms Smith, Mr Smith, Ms Maugham, Mrs Fielding, Mr Fielding, Mr Fielding, Ms Fielding, Mr Smith, Mrs Smith, Mr Borlase,

Ms Dance, Mr Hardwick, Ms Litvinoff, Mrs Litvinoff, Ms Vanessa Bendeth, Mr William Brown, Ms Mary Anne Bennett, Mr Vincent Colley, Ms Jacqueline Butler, Ms Catherine Deacon, Ms Emma Conway, Mr Alexander John Dean, Ms Eileen Abel, Mr Bernard Doherty, Ms Emily Lee, Ms Madelaine Shaw, Mr Harry Harper, Mr Harry Harrison, Ms Sara Hennell, Mr Charles Hill, Ms Sarah King, Mrs Sarah King, Mr John King, Lord Edward Lowe, Ms Marie McCourt, Ms Rebecca Samuels, Ms Nicola Lloyd, Mr Douglas MacDougal, Ms Fiona McLean, Mr David Booker, Ms Freema Agyeman, Mr Jacob Meyer, Mrs Gwyneth Moore, Ms Esau Mwamwaya, Mrs Helen Banks Baker, Ms Elizabeth Geraldine Ballin, Mr John Michael Fletcher, Mr James Joseph Adenuga, Ms Marion Louise Copeland, Mr Derek William Green, Mr John William Lodge, Ms Katherine Anne O'Sullivan, Mr John Corbyn Lind, Ms Suan Brown, Mrs Alison Theresa Mews, all caught on camera coming in and out of and around this shop and around these streets and everywhere they go but we can't hear what they are saying and we can only see them mutely, and we cannot know what they are thinking because they are only images on cameras.

And the voices of the streets, What are you doing over there? and kurwa, daj mi jebane papierosy and no puedo creer lo que me dijo la otra noche en ese bar, fue realmente horrible, ¿lo escuchaste? ¿Dónde estabas en ese momento? Horrible, horrible, simplemente horrible. Dije, hombre, por favor. Sí, sé lo que quieres decir, y luego en el club nocturno, ¿escuchaste lo que dijo? Y ven a los baños. ¿En qué mundo está? And Давай, пойдем в Букингемский дворец, я хочу увидеть чертову королеву и принцессу Маргарет. О чем вы говорите, принцессы Маргарет умерли много лет назад. Реально когда? Много лет назад and Wir könnten heute Abend zu einer Show gehen. Was soll das, ich kann nicht genug Englisch, um zu verstehen, was los ist. Nun, wir könnten vielleicht zu einer der Musikshows gehen, den Musicals, mit einem großen Spektakel und viel Licht und Farben. Wir könnten, könnten wir? And 在那邊。　德國人。　我可以通過它的聲音來判斷。　我敢肯定德國人或者荷蘭人。　聽起來就是這樣。and その写真を撮らなければなりません。　何？　それか？　どうして？　良い感じ。　それは何でもありません。　どうして知っていますか？　知っている。　それはいいですね。　まあ、それのように。　あなたが望むならそれの写真を撮ってください、私はあなたを止めません。　なぜあなたはいつもこれをするのですか？　何をするって？　この。　この。　この？　はい、これ。and To pieprzone życie. Czy możemy się strącić, szefie? Skończyłem na dzień. Zawsze to samo. Zawsze tak samo, za każdym razem. Mówi to, skaczemy do. Zawsze to samo. Nie mogę już dłużej znieść ciebic i twoich jęków. Daj mi papierosy. Daj mi je? Nic nie zostało. Idziemy i kupujemy więcej! And Jeez, did you see that? This guy comes running and four cops are on his tail. Did you see it? Yeah. The black dude. Comes out of nowhere running and like four cops are suddenly coming from four separate directions. Come on, two. OK, two, but they just seemed to be like coming from everywhere and they are bearing down on that black dude, bearing down on him. Yeah? Yeah. Wonder what he done? Nothing, most likely and Taigi aš sakau jam, kad sakau: tu niekur nepasieksi taip elgdamasis ožiuku, jei suprasi, ką aš turiu galvoje.

And the one man up near the bridge reciting, 'Oh, teeming *city*, city full of *dreams*! Where at midday the shadow *walks* and *speaks*! Mighty *colossus*, but with veins that are narrow, my story flows like rising sap *flows*!' shouting as his words fly away in the wind.

And somewhere, elsewhere, there is always another elsewhere, more elsewheres in London, just a few streets over, or a mile away, in the north or the south or the west or east, in the next street to where we are now, there is another here there, another place, another country. Watched by the people in the planes above the city, coming into Heathrow, coming into City, Gatwick, Stansted, commencing their descent. And in the next street, two streets over, we know when we hear the sirens, say, that that is where here is now, for the people there, their here.

3.9

Look, let's be absolutely frank about this story, █████████
██
██
██
██
██
██
██
██
██
██
██
███
██
██
██
████████████████████████████████

Including ████████████████████████████████████
██████████████████

There were also several ██████████████████████████
███████████████ Paul and Julia █████████████████████
██ but
neither could recall.

We can see here that ████████████████████████████
██
██
██

███

██

███████████████████████ It's quite clear that ██████

█████████████████████████████████████

Interview broken off at this point for a two hour recess.

███

████████████████████████████████████

██

███

███

███

███

███████████████ about the two girls. But nothing more.

███

███

███

███

███

███

████████████████████████████████████ Paul.

Julia thinks ████████████████████████████████

███

███

███

███

███

███

███

███████████████

Julia ██████████████████████████████████████

███

███

███

Julia also █████████████████████████████████████

███████████████

██

████████████████

██

██

██

██

███████████████████████████████ saying, 'Surely, you can see that?'

It's hardly as though it could have skipped our minds ███████

██

██

██

██

██

██

██

██

████████████████████████████

██

██

██

██

██

██

██

██

████████████████████████ concluding, that really is all there is to it.

Finally, ████████████████████████████████

████████████████

██

██

██

██

██

██

██

Are we clear, now?

3.10

On a first visit your eye can't help but roam over the tastefully muted colours of the walls, of the skirting boards, of the large rug in the wide, short and low-ceilinged hall. On one side you note deep drawers, in dark-painted medium-density fibreboard, with handles of dull chrome. Above these, paintings of the image of a horse, the *Waverley* ferry sailing 'doon the watter' of the Forth of Clyde and a lighthouse on Skye directs the eye to muslin voiles hanging on thin, white, dusty metal hooks, which falteringly close only with a tug of the hands. You see the rug and floorboards end and a terracotta tile floor begin, naked and buffed.

Now your eye scans an open space of eight metres by three metres. To the right, in front of a disused chimney breast, are two small armchairs of pristine white chenille and again medium-density fibreboard shelves holding ornaments carefully arranged and displayed. Over on the other wall there's a small relief map of Scotland, too small to see the detail of from here. In front of you there is a large, high-backed couch and a rough Bakhtiari Garden carpet on the floor, seemingly held in place by small white hooks like on the rail for the muslin voiles; two dark-red leather easy chairs, parallel to the couch; then a chunky set of mango-wood bookshelves in distressed white, neatly displaying books of all sorts: fiction and non-fiction; cooking and gardening; travel guides; a *World Atlas of Wine*; a *Larousse*; both old and new Vintage Classics, Pelicans; paperbacks and hardbacks; old and new first editions. In front of you here in a recess, piled one on top of the other are old tape cassettes and CDs, a CD player and an amp with, it might seem, too many buttons and lights; and on the floor, propped up against a wall, a colourful canvas capturing the moment of fireworks going off above the Edinburgh Military Tattoo. In a blocked-off wall space of bare brick, a sill still running along the bottom, there's a picture of an empty rural scene. You see a 1928 architect's table in teak and a large metal stool, devoid of any drawing implements. Two mobile phones, seven various chargers, an uncountable tangle of in-ear headphones, a Samsung Galaxy Tab 7.0 and a Kindle DX International sit on a shelf by the door. Below a window sits a square, tall set of free-standing shelves, painted a dull orange, holding sparsely spaced ceramic ornaments, to the side of a circular iroko worktop with a stainless-steel mounting and high stand, with four leather-topped stools arranged around it, bringing the eye again to the muslin voiles.

Colours of chestnut, reds, sky and baby blues – deep and rich, sometimes incongruous, almost seeming thrown together – prevail, with dark hues creeping in elsewhere – a Joan Miró-inspired fabric pattern here, the colour-matched red-, orange- and blue-spined books there. At night, a space that is too dark and low-lit; in the morning and afternoon the windows of the Victorian shell of the house cause revealing shafts of unusual light. And in the summer, this effect – on ornaments, CD spines, high iroko worktop and stools, glints from the stainless steel, small pools of light, and thrown shadows on the floors and walls, the marble kitchen worktops, thin muslin, stainless steel, chenille – make this seem like the beautiful life, the Sunday supplement life.

At last we reach the next room, which again has wooden floorboards and rugs. A French queen-size is here, near the door, and at each side, low and wide bedside cabinets with a comb on one and a watch and ring-holder holding three rings on the other, alarm clocks and small lamps on both, and then books lying here and there. I silently indicate to you to open up bedside cabinet drawers, look inside. Look inside. Along one wall, freshly green-painted medium-density fibreboard doors are built in, and a leather Eames recliner is in front and just to the side of these. In the en suite I point out and we can see light dressing gowns; chrome fittings; our reflections – those people who are us through a small, wall-mounted looking-glass, stare back at us. There's a Braun electric shaver and separate beard trimmer; toothbrushes; perfumes; deodorants; shampoos; conditioners; shower gels; bath gels; handwash and body washes; hair waxes and beard waxes. Simple emulsion whitewash and white eggshell skirting and woodwork; everywhere white Egyptian cotton for towels and sheets and duvet. Back in the room, on a set of shelves, sits a large sphere light, an old tape cassette-radio player and a Kindle 1. The bed's headboard is solid, padded and plaid patterned. Light floods in from the street, and shadows are forming and lengthening. Under the bed are dust and books and a few forgotten things, and there in the en suite an unassuming, short, wide, colourful painting of a fish somehow seems to you, and to I, too prosaic, informal and imperfect.

The next room is mostly empty. We pad softly in to this room. There are shelves, but these seem to serve no purpose. There are a few postcards – Susan Alison MacLeod's *The Mythopoeia of Christ*, a detail from *Christ of Saint John of the Cross*, one of Escher's never-ending staircases, a portrait by Jeremy Andrews, a Kandinsky sketch, a sepia-tint photograph of boys in Glasgow by Oscar Marzaroli, Jenners in Edinburgh, J.B. Yeats' portrait of W.B. Yeats – Sellotaped or Blu-Tacked to the wall. Far off to the right is a short plastic set of drawers for holding stationery with a melted LP record moulded into a bowl shape on top next to an empty square plain white plastic lidded container. In front of a large window there's a low-slung sofa. Yet the feeling of emptiness predominates. No objects that give away the purpose or function of this room. A desktop computer is present, but it is on the exposed floorboard floor, keyboard and mouse stacked up against the monitor, gathering dust. There's a wide chair, right here in front of us, but you couldn't sit down on it, as it is stacked high with patterned pillows and throws, designs by Miró, Mondrian, Kandinsky, Klee, Picasso, Matisse. Other plastic objects seem to have form but no function: art objects; perhaps the unrecognisable out-of-context bits and pieces of large- and medium-sized children's toys. Upstairs are the children's bedrooms and another bathroom. A lovely house, a pleasant home.

The beautiful life, the Sunday supplement life. A simple life, gratifying, satisfying. Deliveries of takeaways when cooking in the cramped, dark galley kitchenette, where there's never enough storage or worktop space, could not be faced. In late June, in the evenings, is when the house is most alive.

After the school run they potter and dawdle, smoking at the back door past the kitchen, or in the back yard. They work from home for a while, then eat at home or go out for something to eat at a coffee shop, usually the independent one, but Starbucks when the independent one was closed.

3.11

Always neat but always informal, comfortable, liveable. It was just the way they lived, comfortably, creatively, thoughtfully. They're on their laptops, listening to CDs, or just chatting quietly to each other. Dinner's after the kids have eaten in front of their screens, having no interest, now, in sitting down with them. Sometimes they all go out for pizza together.

You can see, can't you, a life like this could go on undisturbed, always neat, always comfortable, Sunday supplement photogenic, always beautiful, as though this life were made for them. Of course, they could walk away at any point, sell up and move anywhere, travel the world for a year or two, live near the beach in Costa Rica, perhaps, or visit Machu Picchu: their own family gap year.

As we are watching them, it might be hard almost not to go looking for the peculiarity of this marriage, the peculiarity, the unhappiness, the tension, the edge: where would we look? Maybe in the kitchen cupboards? The bedside cabinets? The bookshelves? Maybe the knickers and pants drawers? Under the bed? A million places. A million details. But which is the detail that counts? This? This? This? This? This? These? This? These? This? These? This? This? This? Or this? Or this? Or even this? Or this? Or this? Or even these? Or this? Or this? These? These? What else? This? This? This? The million details.

It's so obvious, so obvious to us all, anything is possible. Free and in control; comfortable to go, comfortable to stay. A simple and beautiful life.

Come on, along here. We have the time to look around, leaving for now the upper floor, the girls' domain, closer inspection in the hall, see, behind the front door, the unruly pile of posters, leaflets and placards – most, if not all, of which have the word, or perhaps words, ORGAN:EYES somewhere. Professionally-printed placards reading ORGAN:EYES THE EYES OF THE WORLD ARE ON YOU; an amateur placard in a child's painted hand reading ORGANEYES OUR EYES ARE WATCHING; ORGAN:EYES WE WATCH, WE SEE; SCRUTINEYES PARLIAMENT; and again, a child's painted script on a placard reading ORGANEYES WE ARWE WATCHING! THE WORID IS WATCHING! Repeated often, a diagrammatic faceless head with index and middle fingers of a schematic right hand pointing one finger at each place where eyes should be, then the same faceless head with index and middle fingers pointing at the viewer of the image. I make the gesture for you. You understand.

Go along the bookshelves slowly, methodically; you'll notice the mixed and eclectic reading, you'll notice the preponderance of certain books, due to the number by one author: here, Anthony Burgess and Joseph Conrad; there, Yukio Mishima, Flann O'Brien, Georges Perec and Anne Rice; here, books by or about Trotsky, Lenin, Stalin, Voltaire, Orwell; there, books by Dr Seuss, Hergé, Lewis Carroll, Mark Twain and Jack London; higher up, books by Hugh MacDiarmid, Lewis Grassic Gibbon and the Ossian texts; higher up still, the novels in translation of Romain Gary and Émile Ajar; on a shelf to themselves, books by Pablo Neruda and Tristan Tzara and Tom Stoppard; and then, lying off the shelves, casually tossed under a chair or elsewhere, books by John le Carré, Elena Ferrante, Richard Bachman, Woody Allen. A pattern would be emerging. You don't get it yet? Come on, think. There you go. Every one a *nom de plume, nom de guerre*, stage name, alias, *cadre* names, nickname, code name, whatever you want. Pseudonymisation. You have to follow the clues. A giveaway? A simple trick? You're finally getting the hang of this.

Look. How happy they are. A family like many others. Normal people doing normal things normally. Or, rather, no one's normal – normal's not the right word. Jesus. If you've seen the things I've seen. No normal, I tell you. Natural. Natural people doing natural things naturally. Natural people, people at ease in their environment, their world, people, you can see, at home in their own skins. See? People who know who they are. You think? Their north London home at all the times we've been round here, at this time in the evening, on the 24th of June – make a note. It's just before eight – make the note – the lazing informality of bare feet or sloppily falling apart slippers they wear at home. The mother and the youngest daughter are in the parents' bedroom, the mother lying up in bed, legs slipped into the turned-down bedspread and quilt, reading her Kindle, Elena Ferrante. The youngest daughter across the foot of the bed, lying on her stomach, her legs swaying half time in the air to the music coming from her iPad through pink headphones into her ears, Sugababes.

3.12

Through at the dining table, a long oblong of rough-hewn laminate elm atop a repurposed IKEA frame, the eldest daughter sits in the pool of light from a lowered long-wired, circular, brown ceiling lampshade, wearing glasses, her hair tied high at the back, doing her homework, her father leaning over and into the pool of light to see what she's stuck on as she says, 'No, it's not this I was asking about.'

'Oh?'

'No, it was what one of the teachers was saying today about subatomic particles. It's not homework.'

'Really?'

'Yes. I don't really get it.'

'What?'

'Well, she was saying, down at a subatomic level… Well, like there's protons and neutrons and electrons, right?'

'Isn't that atomic level?'

'Yes, right, spot on, Dad. But even at that level we know mostly it's like fresh air… Not fresh air, you know what I mean, vacuum – nothing between these teeny particles, and electrons especially, just flying around in nothing, mostly nothing, oceans of nothing in comparison to the teeny, tiny boat on the ocean that the electrons are.'

'Nice image, very good image.'

'Thanks. So, right, anyway, the teacher was saying today that at the subatomic level there are even tinier component parts of protons and neutrons and electrons, particles literally insanely small in vast, vast... I don't know, galaxy-sized spaces of vacuum, literally nothingness.'

'Okay. I'm hanging on in there.'

'And at this quantum level, it's insane, we are basically vacuum with these teeny, tiny, literally...'

'And what is it that's bothering you about all this?'

'...and I mean, sub-quantum level! Particles that just come into existence and then disappear!'

'Yeah, that's the Large Hadron Collider stuff, isn't it?'

'And the teacher, she says we can't be sure where anything is or whether it's there or not.'

'Is that what they call the Uncertainty Principle? I've never been, you know, certain.'

'I think so.'

'And you said this was bothering you? How is it all bothering you?'

'See what I'm saying? See what I'm saying? I literally *feel* solid. But I'm not. At a quantum level I don't know where anything is! How can I feel *solid*? It's barely there. There's nothing there.'

'You'll get this in life, kid. Sometimes the facts of life will just blow your mind!' His tone is mocking. His daughter sits still, open-mouthed. 'I mean, it will. It will literally blow a gasket in your mind.'

'I just don't get it,' Liv says, as she stares down at her unbelievable arm.

3.13

Look through that kitchen drawer. A what? A letter from the Right Honourable Emily Thornberry MP? And their marriage certificate? Let me read it. 'Mr & Mrs Paul Dorian, 18 Moon Street, Apt. 18, London, United Kingdom, N1 0QU' and says 'THE CITY OF NEW YORK, OFFICE OF THE CITY CLERK, MARRIAGE LICENSE BUREAU, License Number,' and the licence number, 'Certificate of Marriage Registration, This Is To Certify That Paul Dorian residing at 18 Moon Street, Apt. 18, London, United Kingdom, N1 0QU born on 03/10/1964 at Glasgow, United Kingdom and Julia Smith residing at 18 Moon Street, Apt. 18, London, UNITED KINGDOM, N1 0QU born on 01/27/1966 at Manchester, United Kingdom Were Married on 03/10/2005 at Office of the City Clerk, 1 Centre Street, NYC, NY 10007 as shown by the duly registered license and certificate of marriage of said persons on file in this office. CERTIFIED THIS DATE AT THE CITY CLERK'S OFFICE Manhattan NY, March 11, 2005. PLEASE NOTE: Facsimile Signature and seal are printed pursuant to Section 11-A, Domestic Relations Law of New York.' Then the seal, then the signature of Victor L. Robles, then, 'Victor L. Robles, City Clerk of the City of New York.' What else? All the paperwork from the eldest daughter's baby months, toddler years and early childhood? I see. Noting that the eldest didn't get immunised for MMR, and she developed measles at age five just as the second kid was born. She developed pneumonia, was hospitalised in Edinburgh, the Western Infirmary, and then the Royal Hospital for Sick Children. The paperwork for the second child seems to be missing from the drawer; perhaps it has never quite made it to this archive status and it is in some technically live file, that discarded Cath Kidston bag, under the stairs. The father now kicks off his shoes, his sensible pair of black Loake Actons, the ones he feels he must wear to his job in the charity. Not the Docs and Converse of the life side of his work/life balance that sit amongst the posters and placards behind the front door. Show me that. A lanyard that was lying by his side tells us the charity combats homelessness. Back through in the bedroom the mother receives a text from a colleague, which reads, 'All OK with thedoc/policy leaving office now FINALLY.' Her lanyard, lying on the dressing table of the parents' bedroom, notes her work is with a campaign group for rape crisis and domestic violence services. Have a look yourself.

It's about to be eight o'clock and the Channel 4 News has just ended.

The mother has moved upstairs to her ten-year-old daughter's bedroom and has fallen asleep in her bed beside her, a brush still in her hand. She was about to brush or had been brushing out her daughter's long hair. By the look of her, she is wiped out; like it has been a long week and she's still unwinding. The father and his fifteen-year-old daughter, having given up on her homework, are sitting on the couch, curled up together.

'Do you want to listen to some Beefheart?'

She gives him *the teenage look of death*. Now they're watching television and chatting about subatomic particles.

'Do you think you understand it?'

'People don't like indeterminacy. Like that thing that happened a while back, in the Met Police, you could be clean-shaven or have a beard, but you couldn't be seen to be just unshaven.'

'What?'

'I mean, a copper who looks, you know, scruffy, couldn't be bothered… Just no, you know, authority. Clean, fine. Beard, fine. Authority. Anything else, no authority…'

'What *are* you talking about?'

'I'm just saying, in transition…'

'I was talking about particles.'

'Well, yeah, at a subatomic level, they say, don't they, that we're only approximations of ourselves.'

'Hm. Yes. That sounds about right.'

'Hey, watch this.' Paul stretches over and grabs the deck of cards from where they are sitting and on the coffee table in front of them does two splits and a ripple. He deals two cards for Liv. She looks at them without moving, then, when he turns to her, she sighs, sits forward, and turns them over. The Jack of clubs and the Ace of diamonds.

'Is that it?'

Paul deals another two cards. 'Go on, they're yours as well.'

Liv turns the two cards. The Jack of spades and the Ace of spades. 'Mm.'

'Now watch this.' Paul deals five cards, turns them over.

'So?'

'Count them up. Five card trick. Four, nine, three, seventeen, eighteen, nineteen, twenty, twenty-one. Five card trick and a twenty-one, too.'

Liv starts moving back into position, slouching on the couch, gathering a blanket around herself. 'Yeah, but Dad, the point is you manipulate the cards, but, well, so what? You know what I mean?'

'Huh? It's just a trick.'

'It's just cheating. The point of a game of cards is the element of chance. If you can do what you can do, cheat, there's no point in ever playing cards at all, is there? You won't let the game be what it is.' She settles herself back into the space her body was before, except his shoulder, which her head had been leaning on, isn't there. A few minutes later he's still sitting forward, looking at the cards. 'Actually, I'm going to bed.' She gathers herself together, ready to go.

'OK, goodnight.' Then he looks up at her because she's looking down at him.

'And, anyway, both twenty-ones I got had black Jacks in them. I won.' She turns and walks to the stairs, trailing the blanket behind her and leaving the house quiet.

In the quiet of the house after eight, Paul stretches out on the couch, his bare feet up on the coffee table, his head back. The brush lolls in Julia's hand, a sudden feeling of weight and falling that wakens her, but she keeps her eyes closed. Sophie is lying next to her mother, watching her. Liv lies up on her bed in her bedroom, the blanket wrapped around her, waiting.

And Julia is thinking, New York and Skye, why together? The Municipal Building, because it's by the authority of City Hall, just not there, looked like a dole office from the eighties, graffiti, we weren't sure Liv could as she was only nine so we asked the lady with the English accent to be, laughing the whole time, the Hawaiian wedding behind us, first come first served basis, garlands et cetera, then the eastern European one behind that, the bride in full bog-roll-holder white. Oh, the greatest day, the most important day of any little girl's life! Well, my wedding day was… Oh, yes, such a dream come true. Here comes the bride. Well, now. Fake. Fakery fake. Fake like the. Like the news.

And Paul is thinking, What was I thinking. Glasgow? The Glasgow School of Art? What was I— yeah, already said. I think it was something about the old man and lady coming from there, Scotland, not Glasgow. Mock Jock. Even in school same thing. Because I would say wee for small. But not in the same or correct or. So fucking what? Khimme a break. When I was a wee boiy. And one time lum for chimney. Almost a kicking subsided into laughter. And having to follow aye as though I had started a sentence I. Are you so and so or such and such and I said aye… am such and such. What else have we disagreed on, me and her? The Arab Spring. What the girls wear, almost in all instances. Regular visits to the dentist. Leveson. Named soon. The achievements of Barack Obama. Ed Miliband. Just, Ed Miliband. The efficacy of entryism into the Labour Party. Whether the girls should share a room to free up space for a music room/playroom/cinema room upstairs. But the one down here. Other things to disagree on. She said men always with their I, I, I. Bloody egotists. Never shut up about our I think this and I think that and this is where I am coming from. I said, and what do women say, and she said they were more self-effacing and they would say you. Like when you have an opinion you would be thinking this and this or you would be thinking that and that. And I said that men can just be honest about thinking when they're thinking that it's their opinion and no one else's. All that you shit is just the imposition of the I opinion on everyone else. When you have a baby. No. Not when *you* have a baby. Are you telling the person who you're talking to that this is how they will feel when *they* have a baby? Fucking fascistic, that. Telling people how they will feel. Men keep it to the honesty of when I had a baby corrected quickly to when we had a baby when my wife had a baby, but still she pounced. Exactly, she said, men don't have babies. Hipster London. The local. The food in the local. Gentrification. Gentrification of this area. Gentrification as noted in the local. Supporting a local Green Party councillor who happens to be a friend Julia has made. The Green Party. The girls' commitment to all things the colour pink. Whether girls reading books should only present strong role models of girls and women or whether books with boy protagonists are okay. (*Harry Potter*.) Palestine. Books. What a load of shit books are. Novels. Fuck's sake. Waste of money, waste of paper. In fact, environmental disaster, all those books, all those trees. Though, Kindles, though. Though, electricity, though. Though, the Internet, though. Though, Amazon, though. Unacceptable face of capitalism.

He can't work his gadgets, Julia's thinking, WhatsApp, told the sender can see when message is picked up he'd been late to do it, like the son of um —— who sees how long his tutor looks at his essay before a grade on a Uni VLE, she said, Jesus, maybe we're all the surveillance of everyone else these days, why does she hide? Sometimes the only trick is to keep breathing. *The Trick is to Keep Breathing*. The Prick, with her kiddie party version of the uniform, Kilburn Road, Liv nine falling asleep at the table in Balthazars, but not really about Skye talking every day about further out, Uist, Harris, Lewis. That one who lived out on Harris. Men are women now, is it? And he looked like he was going to say something one night but then that moment passed on its own and, well, like he said, 'There's nothing *to* tell.' Never did work out what he was doing up there, hiding out? Before the girls, almost two years, I was there because he was, the house in Skye, just inland from the lighthouse, the stairs, very weird, more like a ladder, too big for us, you know why, do I? In the evenings he went outside to watch and smoke. Far away from everything, ourselves. And the time we finally made it to the lighthouse. Come on, who wouldn't? Yes, I know, I could, Elena Ferrante, maybe we all hide, everyone is hiding, we're all hiding, behind the mask, masked ball that time, behind the absence, all, we all know why, because his year at Glasgow School of Art with Douglas, because he's always been a Mock Jock, English through and through but with the Scottish parents so had some freaky strange affinity with Skye of all places, no one knows anything, everything is, tell the truth, it's all lies. Born in Glasgow. Means nothing.

Paul looks at the CD player, but then decides not to play anything. He's thinking, I mean, is dentistry really a mechanism of state control? Israel. The comedy delights of local comedian Stewart Lee. How the structural defects of capitalism manifest themselves most obviously in the local community. The pros and cons of the local schools. The use of a car or van for transport in inner London ('You don't complain when I get everyone everywhere'). *The Colour of Spring* versus *Spirit of Eden*; Bob Dylan; Joni Mitchell; punk; jazz; the hilariousness of Samuel Beckett. Why Stewart Lee would not also be a manager in the local Sainsbury's as opposed to the new manager of the local Sainsbury's just having a passing resemblance to Stewart Lee… *écoute et répète*. Double-barrelled names in relation to the offspring of married and unmarried couples when not actually in the aristocracy. Who the money goes to when we're dead.

I have faith in only one person, Fabius. I can't believe how normal normal can be again.

Julia opens her eyes and looks at Sophie, and they smile. And she's thinking, Then deeper under than SDS disbanded NDEDIU NPIQO all the rest, fronts and backs, crossing London, up the Kilburn Road until we weren't in Kilburn any more, Toto, to look at and order a leather chair and footstool, one of the pleasures of the pre- or is that early-Internet was such voyages of discovery, bon voy a geee!, into an unknown world, a surreal world of sea snails and Nigerian restaurants, that's when, a curious coldness in the? When we came out of the wedding room or whatever you would call it I turned to him and said do you think that lasted more than a minute? Ring? No ring, OK. Maybe embers of a fire that kept you warm at night. May be. The sort of people who, when new people buy a house in the street, we go and introduce ourselves, when a new set of students rent the HMO at the corner, we get to know them so that all can avoid difficulties by emphasising the students' valued part in their neighbourhood. We're good people. It doesn't matter the.

And Paul is thinking, That fizzled out years ago, anyway, and she says she doesn't feel betrayed or violated. The kids being born. 'Who has the perfect circumstances for that anyway? I can't think of any of our friends...' Because anyway the young have a right to say how the world should be in the future and how, yeah, that's their right. Says she's going vegan, save the planet, save the fucking whale, time is getting short, well maybe I'll wait for the four-minute warning we had to think endlessly about when we were kids. TV detector vans. Scare the nation. Surveilling. Surveillancing? Never thought of it that way. They knew. Because it was the BBC, cameras and stuff, seemed likely. But as they are, what they will be willing to do to save the planet, that's the question. Then a pet dog pops up from somewhere and one of the activists is going to appear on TV with this dog and then other activists, sixteen-year-old girls, are saying how cute the dog is, and then about how Soph has been asking over and over, since she was tiny, and Liv has been asking since before that and how if I had got them this dog they wanted and how I would now be convincing them that really, this dog, Rover or whatever, something like that, would have to go, that of course pet animals are a pointless extravagance for a world with global warming, how these animals are just fuel for a house on fire, a particularly pointless fuel for this fire, and our world is on fire, isn't it?

And closing her eyes again Julia is thinking, Leveson, the bathroom cabinet? 'Yeah, knew that would be that way,' or is it something that looks one way and feels like another? Like their names, so... typical, like fakes chosen to conceal some grotesque uniqueness, names like almost absurd attempts to seem like we were just like anyone else, names that looked like we had been chosen from the top baby names for the year before the year of each of our births, Janet and John or Jack and Jill our names and if the daughters were actually called DD1 and DD2 we wouldn't be less absurd.

Sophie looks over at her mother, whose eyes are closed, but she doesn't seem asleep. And Sophie is thinking, Literally. If I'm thirsty I tell Liv then it's Aquamentiticamu, ha, the game! And she says is that from the books or you are making it up I can't remember and I say it's a spell, my spell, I show her just with a finger, of swishing a wand in front of her and Ascendididioso! (to fly upwards myself or herself, what a trick!) or Levitaticorpuschristi! (to have someone, an opponent, hoisted up into the air by the ankle, ankle?, ankle), Titanium, and telling Liv about Katy Perry. I *like* to change them a bit, I said.

Paul's thinking, But, really, baby, don't you see? It's Rover. Telling a billion teenage boys and girls that it's Rover and Fluffy that are part of the problem *not* the solution, and I'm sorry but Fluffy and Rover, pulls gun from holster, well, Rover's just gotta go. Dupe teenage girls. Dupes of the Left. Causing the nervous breakdown of a generation of these young girls, a mass breakdown event, and the end of days, the death that is nigh. Yes,

Daddy, I can see why Rover has to go, and yes, that's it, that actually here starts a mass movement of teenage girls who live to kill first their own pets and then anyone else's pet that they can get their bloodied hands on because the pets are the problem, don't you see, and we have to do what is needed.

In her bed, staring at the ceiling, Liv is thinking, Because have to leave at a moment's notice all my life. Both of them. Well, we'll see. Because I'm going to grab Sophie and then. Soon as I'm eighteen though need to check if I'd be allowed. Because would I be? O wonder! How many goodly creatures are there here! How beauteous mankind is! O brave new world that has such people in't. So bloody pleased with himself. Performing monkey. Smiling there like.

And Julia is thinking, 'I won't be happy until you're as unhappy as I am,' maybe, to keep a marriage going, you have to use every trick in the book, or maybe you just let things lie, in the hall by the door, the banners from, the furniture from IKEA kept that little bit too, like student days never ended, the expensive Persian rug that was an indulgence when we were DINKies, double income, no kids, there are other extravagances from that time, too, his electric guitar (never really learned to play, a beautiful black Fender Telecaster USA, he loves the smell of the case's crushedish velvet interior, the way the case's interior's crushedish velvet cradles that guitar), of course I fucking knew his job isn't much of a real job at all, that some of his trips abroad are for the charity. There's no way to bring nutjob conspiracy theorists back from the brink. There's only one way to fuck them up. Introduce a conspiracy to the, incept it, that does them all in, Jonestown-, Branch Davidian-style. 'The apocalypse is upon us' is always the best one. Trannies when I was growing up were transistor radios. Then they were transvestites. Now where are we? I mean you can't, can you. Rapists in the toilet?

And Sophie is thinking, Oh my gosh. The panic room. And he literally always has a crappy phone, Liv says. Always cheap phones. She hates that. 'Not the crappy phone! Not *another* crappy phone!'

Her room. Literally playing the Harry Potter Game. Making those jokes up. Mugs in Ollllllllllivaaaaanders. Lordy Vuldimurt, Valdimart, Veldumert, Vildumirt. The Squirrell. Deaf Eatahs. Eatahs! Aquament. Nuncimorium! Comedentillud! The Expulsoitium! that gave you away. Effundiatis. Hairy and Run. Lumost Minimaximosa. Baggort shapesshifters. Wingdingardium Levitiparamosa. Lost my Ripping Ch-harm, Bobble-Heed Ch-harm. Alohohohohhomo-momomorarara. Slughohehahihuhorn. Gilderilderoy Loveheart. Playing with Liv. Basically last time she.

And Paul is thinking, Say to her. We live in an oligarchy of Oxbridge graduates, and thank fuck for that. Can you imagine what actual democracy would look like? Fuck me. The people have spoken, the bastards. Jesus, if it wasn't for the nobs in parliament and government we'd be bringing back hanging and legalising the stoning of nonces. Expenses scandal, nose in the trough. Smashing the faces of Emily and Nadine to a pulp, that would not get old, get them down the custody suite. Fucking claiming rent on houses they own, section 17 of the Theft Act 1968. Cleaning a fucking moat. Fucking midget Hazel rocking the boat. Read the writ, false accounting. And loads of Barons from the Lords. Keeping up the name of Robber Bastards, I guess.

And Liv is thinking, Brave new world what has such people, innit? Hehe. Get in 'the population it requires'. Lenina Crowne and Bernard Marx, supping on the Soma... when asked say career ambitions dum de dum Resident World Controller. AF632 is AD 2540 and written in 1931, so Huxley reckons about 610 years to go from historical figure to possible messiah.

And Sophie is thinking, PlayStation but not the Wii, so basically I'm running through streets corridors rooms Roblox, Sugababes, waiting for it on iOS, Charts, is it? Literally the catchiest songs, in game? YouTube? And then Liv says.

Dad's joke about Douglas being a messiass, Liv's thinking. Enough forgetting and losing and misplacing and misinterpreting, 600 years?

And Paul is thinking, The liberal priest who Julia likes. Beggars. Priests and ministers. Experts in 16th century French poetry who demand you fix their palatial residences, pay them salaries, pay their travel expenses as they travel round the world, pay for their holidays, their clothes, their cars, and if they're ministers or pastors, pay for their stupid spouses and kids to do the same stupid shit as themselves.

And Julia thinks she may get up and go down to her own bed, as her mind wanders. She's thinking, Brocade, there's a complexity to Enoch Powell, he closed the old asylums, that was kind of a progressive thing to do, and if you bother to read or listen to the whole thing the whip hand comment was a quote from one of his constituents that he said he was duty bound to respond to, he saw rivers of blood classical reference of course well anyway what she was saying in May, May in May, that she wanted a really hostile environment and even Labour say it too something like it, bring it down, it's all just culmination of Enoch, saying Enoch wasn't wrong, Enoch Was Right t-shirts, culmination, maybe Theresa May, maybe Theresa May Not, may be. Farage Was Right, How about that? Farage Is Right, stupid twats forgot to put the bloody name on the paper, but none of them can say otherwise that it's hostile environment, Farage doesn't even have to, quite bloody right, too, I mean, you can't have them all coming, it's just common sense, it's interesting listening to the Luton boy, he makes it a bit clearer each time, it's not this, it's this, not that, but this, like he's thinking about it and coming to better conclusions, I'll give him that, but we can't be, it's common sense, too, so, where's the common in common sense? There, the information coming through about an occupation movement. New York. Wall Street. City Hall, the Municipal Building, social media is going to make a fucking riot much easier, but it is common sense, she is, I mean, watch her for any length of time, Leveson Inquiry, no doubt, she can't hold a look, looking at her, her looking at us, can watch her hurt brain looking around even if her eyes aren't for that screen,

She relates to, prefers it to us, and you can watch her as the little dopamine receptors get a battering, light, colour, sound, Ping, Ping, Ping, we're just fuzzy objects in the background, I told him, bloody MMR, Wakefield, all proven, her little arm and that bloody needle, and the others, all of them, 'Look,' I said, 'Vitamin K is different, whole different story,' music in her ears, it's all just to block us out, and you could watch it all happening, soon as she got them, common sense, an effect every time, and he said it's just not happening, and he thinks I know nothing about him, well, not now, but before, and the other things he hides, I know there isn't some wife out there but he has parents, I know, I wonder what he still believes about me? All of the other stuff, bloody common sense, Leveson, I mean, and who the hell gets infectious diseases anyway these days? I mean, what is vaccination for?

And as though they were thinking of similar things, Julia and Paul, he's thinking, Just damaging kids? Their soft little brains? Hers? Epidemics, I mean, well, swine flu, grannies, not much, SARS, people in China wearing face masks like nutters, and all for what? Autism, Jesus, if only they bloody knew, and also, The Prick getting her bauble QPM and she'll keep getting stuff like that and failing upwards, old Private Dick, up to her neck in the way he got shot, I was told, it was all over, she'll end up top cat, Jesus, all of the other stuff, The Prick, who said it? Good one, one of the good ones, protects his own, come a time with the cameras and all that and everyone will be going around like fucking bandits, swag bags and faces covered.

Sophie is thinking, Any time of day, can't, why they sing that, on the line, Liv says it's a can't remember the word, when she's eighteen she says, because by then we literally won't need them. Cause we can. Be a bit freaky. Freakiness. Just like me. Because basically first there was Siobhan and Mutya and Keisha but then Siobhan left and Heidi joined but then Mutya left and Amelie joined, but then Keisha left and Jade joined and I guess that's the point at which you would say that basically Sugababes weren't really Sugababes any more.

And Julia is thinking, Maybe all marriages are unhappy, maybe all marriages are built on a rock, a huge boulder that has to be rolled uphill each day classical reference and the rock is this: but I know that he's not always travelling for them, sometimes he's just taking a holiday to himself, and sometimes he's not even abroad at all, Diane von Furstenberg dresses (three), genteel semi-poverty, if you can call it anything, though the way the money seems to come from somewhere inexplicably when needed, it was that that should have told him though the grandparent cull was also, the girls never knowing their grandparents at all, but they think this is a normal state of affairs, they think, Who *are* these old people other girls hang around with?

Sounds about OK, Liv's thinking. Jesus did it in, what, a hundred? Even the contemporary well anyway never mind.

And Paul is thinking, I know secretly she takes communion. Confession. Jesus. The number of times I was going to. Just tell her everything. That night on Skye. Because something about the sunset. And we were miles from where we were then. Because I was looking at her and maybe that's when I was thinking, this isn't too bad, not too bad at all. She was looking. Love? A dog came barking across the machair. Still they have their uses. Want to creep round yer neighbourhood at night and not be thought a sinister bastard? Get yourself a mutt. I never bothered. I am sinister. That time I said to Sally. She said, 'Have you met Ivan?' Ivan was the dog. I said, 'Well, I've been in the same room as the dog the owner calls Ivan. I don't know so much about "met".' Probably hurt her feelings. Ah well. Khimme a break, like he used to say. Even when I was creeping around my neighbourhood, seeing shadows in the bushes, people in the shadows. Heart thumping, jumping out of my skin, seeing eyes everywhere. The way she says that Soph won't. Asperger syndrome, please. I mean, just a kid like a kid, into her own thing. She's bright, is what. Way she devoured *Harry Potter*. Others. But it was probably just dog walkers and their mutts pissing or shitting, or them pissing and shitting. Illusion vs. delusion. Plausible. 20.20, 21.21, 22.22, 23.23. Memory playing tricks. In the newspapers today they are saying cars and factories shutting down is just not going to cut it for global warming and we should all consider going vegetarian and think about land use. Well, A causes B, B causes A, or C causes A and B to happen in some relation to each other. Thing is, C is so often hidden. And I suppose A and B may not be causal at all. Christ, London like a tinderbox. You can *smell* it coming. A couple of years and us rozzers will all be wearing gang colours, a black flag, or a blue one, or a black one with a blue line on it. Christ. London in flames.

And Liv is thinking, The way I have to wake up every day at 7:00 AM to the sound of his waking-up farts, to the smell of his waking-up farts. Don't give me that, bought before leather was… upcycled from a skip in one case, it's all just animal, isn't it? 18. Get away from the two of them. Not to be trusted. Money in my and other money in my. The stink. The stink of the two of them. The stink of their cigarettes and their leather chairs. The eye that surveys the I, the watcher inside the self that sees all. To him, to me, to everyone. There's always been a bit of him in that eye. He was watching. Him. He's watching me. It's always with me, even now.

And Paul is thinking, So, my idea about sending death squads to the poorest nations still not cutting it. The well-thumbed copy of *Chavs* by Owen Jones – you have to know your enemy (Channel 4 News, the *Guardian*, all that) – says next a how-to guide to enable me, my daughters, their children, to ingratiate themselves as far as possible into the Establishment. Up the arses of the Establishment. For them to accrue as much power, secret power, in society as possible. O one daughter an MP, Minister of State, the other a judge or QC. Soph going to nail it, the Asperger syn coming in handy then if that's what it is. Old Marx, he got it right but didn't realise all the implications of what he was saying when he said all property is theft (not actual quote by Marx), because what that means is that if you want anything, if you want a piece of what there is, then you got to nick it, take it, by force, grab it from the nearest weakest person. And that's what we all do. Aristocracy. Church. Fucking bankers, Canary Wharf types. KTs. All. Evening, all. Long arm of the law. Thin blue line. All that. The walls around the haul. For them. Yeah, well for me too, then. That's what that means. Of course, because MI6 want me now, international criminal activity, I'll be immune to prosecution. From. Immune. Vaccine. Vaccination. Vaxxers. Anti-vaxxers. And now the TERFs and the transers are going for each others' throats and I'm just glad that for once I literally do not have skin in the game. I don't even care. She's a TERF, though, that's for sure. Her age. Men are in her book. Homeopathy, she says. Soph. If you've done nothing wrong, you've nothing to fear. Yeah, and when all the cameras are pointing at us? Have we never done nothing wrong? When the big one comes. They'll all die out. Didn't get the vax. Her. Yeah, well, maybe the truth is we don't live in that culture. Maybe the horrible truth is we live in a culture where young women and some young men have become so confused by relationships they see the only way forward from a bad relationship is taking the other person to court charged with it. Non-binary, too, I suppose. What about that, eh? Maybe cases are failing left, right and centre because it's just all not happening. There are no 95% walking free. Trans people. What? There's just 95% of false accusations. This phone business. What would an alleged victim have to fear if they weren't trying to hide something, anyway? O, the whole system is stacked against them. Sure. Or against the alleged perpetrators. Ever thought about that?

And Liv is thinking, Exploited animals. Ugh. Animal skin. Because disgusting. And they smell of it when they've been sitting in them all day. Stink of it and the cigarettes even if they do smoke out in the back yard.

And Paul is thinking, The courts are our best way of sorting that out. What if the conviction rate is right? I might have been working in this bullshit policing for too long now, but I've worked in real policing too, and that we have an epidemic is equal bullshit. Crisis. Crisis. The mental health crisis. The autism epidemic. All bullshit. I've met more freaks and weirdos than you've had hot dinners, mate.

And Liv is thinking, The ashtrays in the house may now remain for ever empty, but the whole back yard is just one big ashtray and they stink of it. Because the stink of them. His stink. Their stink. His feet. They don't stink but they're just *there*. And anyway, she said, 'The eyes of God may or may not be upon your soul, but the rest of you is definitely within sight of Google Earth.' God, how I loathe him when he does that voice. So false. Hate him. I just don't get it.

They were always around, Paul's thinking, as he makes his way to bed. There just isn't more of them now. There just isn't. I look at Liv. Is she mine? Looks nothing like me. Know what I'm saying? All her. Julia. They said use your real name, it simplifies things. MMR, Wakefield. Got her shitting herself. I told you so, she said. What did I tell you? All my fault of course because the time with Liv had me shitting myself. You made me get them for Soph and look at her now. She's no more autistic than I am or a hole in the ground. Tell you what I can't tell her. Heard it from a couple of them. It's all the fucking NCT, doulas, waterbirth bullshit. Birth trauma through the roof. Kids not getting oxygen. Even midwife-led in the maternities. Dithering. Not getting the kids out. Nothing to do with MMR or any other. That's what the hippies don't want to hear. That they're the cause of it. Boris Johnson for London again and the fucking UKIP forgot. She likes Farage but doesn't. Then there was the time I was standing in a doorway and the man whose doorway it was arriving home around one in the morning and looking at me. I straightened, stiffened, but I stayed where I was as the man opened the door and goes in to the house only to re-emerge a few moments later and says, 'Sorry, friend, but you know this is my house and I've got to wonder.' I nodded.

Acknowledged that it was a fair point and that I'll go in a moment. But then looking at the man I don't know why but I said, 'It's just,' then I looked over at the flats opposite, 'my girlfriend. That's the flat of some bloke from work she's out with in a gang… from work.' 'Right,' said the door owner, 'and you think maybe she'll arrive back with him maybe? And tell you she stayed over with one of the girls?' 'She doesn't even have to do that,' I said. 'We don't live together.' Followed her a couple of times to places in other circumstances when we did live together, but not since the kids came along. God, that racket. Because Pat Nevin. Because Chelsea. When all I ever want to listen to is Cocteau Twins. Fell to pieces not because of the the. And the. But because they had run out of making the blissed-out melodies. Every single one, every possibility. Just gone through them all. World goes vegan for animal lovers have to slaughter all the farm animals. Maybe not what they were thinking of. And the pets. Big slaughter, too? Do vegans have pets? Sounds a bit exploity, that. Using them to be your friend. Keeping them a lifetime. Sounds worse than just eating the fuckers, actually. When I allowed myself to eat meat in front of her. That first holiday together. Chania. The apartment we had, up two flights of stairs within a courtyard, something like one anyway, just behind the marina. High window. 'Let Down'. I want my furry animals on the David Attenborough Show, don't give a fuck about the locals want to kill it all to live off groundnut oil profits. Extra cred points. And I suddenly was thinking oh fuck, I'm actually going to throw myself down. She was through in the bedroom sleeping. That was the first time, too. The stress getting to me. Something wrong. The first. First time I realised that I was there for other reasons. Was it her or watching her? Which was it? What was I doing? Why come away on holiday? That was hardly in the manual, not on the training. Sarge ready to kill me finding out I had eaten meat. How did he get to know? Can't remember. Somehow. And not, I want to throw myself down. Oh fuck, I'm going to throw myself down. Just a momentary. Passed. Didn't think about it again for months. Years. But now. It was the first, that's all. Curious feeling. Uncontrolled. Control. What I said to Liv. What I have told her. O how I could smash a brick repeatedly into the face of any Tory woman MP. Or any woman MP. Their self-satisfied knowledge that they're right. Forget women. Any fucking MPs, really. Brick. Smash. Teeth flying. Nose broken fucking bloodied. Because then he said, 'I don't quite understand, then. Who is she to you? I think I lost track.' And I said, 'When it comes down to it, mate, it's not your business.' 'It's my house, it's my door,' he said. 'I get you,' I said, 'I said I'll be gone in a minute.' Flashed the police ID. He said no more, nodded, went inside. I did wait until she got there. Maybe a twinge of. Nah. Not thinking that way, not then, not ever in some real sense. She's just the target. Only societal authority you can gain or at least seek from a fucking washing-up-liquid bottle. Soph, though. Got to keep in mind. Yeah, let's all go vegan, slaughter every fucking farmyard cunt and be done with the whole circus. Oxford, Cambridge, Finsbury, Piccadilly, Westferry, Arnold, Ludgate, Holborn. Fucking clowns everywhere. Know the enemy. Know your enemy.

Liv turns in her bed, pulling the blanket around her, listening for her mother. And she's thinking, When he takes off his shoes and socks and he's barefoot and there they are, thrown up on the coffee table, wriggling toes, toes with hair. Oh for God's sake. Disgusting. Because then he says, Sorry, is it the plates of meat? Because his meaty feet. You've got to understand, Liv, he says. Freedom. We cannot have or demand or take or bestow freedom. There's only control, control of ourselves and others. And you have to decide what part you play in that control. And whether that control is to your advantage, and once you decide how it can be to your advantage, you run with that system of control. At a quantum level? Because I know what control I want, what freedom I want. Because the stink of them when they come in half all in because at lunch they've been eating those greasy chips and the stink of them and the stink of wine stale on their stinking breaths and the two of them for God's sake. Liv, I want you to listen to me, he says. This is the most important thing I'm ever going to say to you. Do you understand? Everybody knows that the price of freedom is eternal surveillance. Eternal surveillance is the price of… um. Too drunk. Because freedom; power is stealing from the many. Freedom is food that must be eaten each day or it rots. Do you see? Think today, forget yesterday. Because the powerful become, either from the failure of being human or the way they stick together because they must, the necessary enemy of the people. He could have been an activist, really, and now he's the filth, and his argument adds up to much the same either way. And remembering her lesson on the American Revolution, she's thinking, Only by continued oversight can those in office be prevented from hardening into despots; only by unremitting agitation can people be sufficiently awake not to let freedom be smothered. Because eternal surveillance is the price of your freedom. Remember it. Pray the guards on the watchtower never sleep or look away. The price of liberty, and even of common humanity, is eternal surveillance. And we have to constantly train and equip and upgrade technology to meet ever-growing and ever-changing challenges. Eternal surveillance is the price for continuing security. In fact, eternal surveillance is not the price of freedom or of security. It's the price of everything. Every object you own has to be protected. There will always be people who oppose and abuse whatever you hold dear. They will try to overrule and evade and weaken you. Others will seek power, wealth, status, they'll use every trick in the book, without doing anything real to earn it. The only way to keep what you have is to guard it constantly. Eternal surveillance is not only the price of liberty; eternal surveillance is the price of human decency.

And Sophie is thinking, But then maybe that happened basically when Siobhan and Heidi swapped or maybe it was when Mutya and Amelie swapped because then there was more replaced than original that being a three to one, three to two I mean, two of three ratio or something, but then Mutya, Keisha and Siobhan could reform now as they're all free but then who would Sugababes be then? And also, the songs I like, really it's Keisha, Mutya and Heidi, but that seems a little unfair on Siobhan, and even on Amelie and Jade, but then it's unfair on all of them really, basically all of them all individually. Maybe they could literally form a six-girl group, then basically literally that would be fair on everyone but then maybe they don't get on I wonder whether it's Jade gets on with Mutya, Keisha and Siobhan and Amelie gets on with Mutya and Siobhan and Mutya, Keisha and Siobhan get on with Jade and Mutya and Siobhan get on with Amelie, because they were never in the group at the same time, yeah, I bet it could literally be like that. The bunker, literally like a panic room, one day can be safe, with or without them, in case, one day, someone came.

And Liv is thinking, I am. I am if it helps you believe what I'm saying, he says. You're frightening me. No. I'm strengthening you. I won't live in fear, and you won't either. We are the watchers, the guards, the winners. Remember that. Because it's Irish lawyer/politician Philpot Curran and frequently to Thomas Jefferson. Dublin. 17 sometime. American Revolution. Topic 12.

And Sophie's thinking, Trying to take me or Liv away, or them away, and she would literally make sure it could not be hacked and she would say through the steel door.

And Liv's thinking, God gives liberty to man conditional on eternal surveillance. Because no evidence to confirm that Thomas Jefferson ever said or wrote anything like it. Context. Next you get the abolitionist Wendell Phillips.

And Sophie's thinking, Literally, Liv says I've to be ready but not what for. Ascend! Levicorp! That would get them, would shout it through the steel door of the panic room really quickly, really loudly, what he was on about anyway, homework, don't want to sit next to him either, need to tell the. Could tell Liv but what could Liv do about it, won't tell them, Liv says not to tell them. And basically they won't need us, I wonder why?

So you can see the way I feel, Liv's thinking. My personal favourite is by the novelist Aldous Huxley. Something that was wrong. Because in his spoken introduction to the 1956 CBS Radio Workshop adaptation of his novel *Brave New World*. Shelter. Hideaway. Please teach me gently how to breathe. Back at you. Mirror images. Be kind. It too. Morning, patient, kind, wasted. Who the hell. Was I? My, my, my. Jasmine Lucilla Elizabeth Jennifer van den Bogaerde. Come on. Who the hell? That's a lot of names. CD out in November, I heard. She's the same age as me, basically. Was twelve when she won the Open Mic. Twelve. Twelve. 'Skinny Love'. My. But then heard the mother is some concert pianist or something. XX. And Bon Iver. Happy winter. Some old TV show. *Dirk*. Be patient. Some old movie star. Last. A year. My, my.

Sophie's thinking, And Liv says she won't have to build a panic room for us because. Because something. I'll ask her again.

And Liv is thinking, Common. Actually this was the homework. American Revolution. They that can give up essential liberty to purchase a little temporary safety, deserve neither liberty nor safety or They that can give up essential liberty to obtain a little temporary safety deserve neither liberty nor safety or Those Who Sacrifice Liberty For Security Deserve Neither or He who would trade liberty for some temporary security deserves neither liberty nor security or He who sacrifices freedom for security deserves neither or People willing to trade their freedom for temporary security deserve neither and will lose both or If we restrict liberty to attain security we will lose them both or Any society that would give up a little liberty to gain a little security will deserve neither and lose both or He who gives up freedom for safety deserves neither or Those who would trade in their freedom for their protection deserve neither or Those who give up their liberty for more security neither deserve liberty nor security. The lesson today is Contextomy.

She'll look after both of us, literally that she can do that, Sophie's thinking. I suppose I'll miss some things but more them than them. Literally.

At the bottom of the stairs we look up into darkness and wonder. Look, I don't really care about your reservations. We've come this far. Now is the time to sort this out, to find out what there is to find out.

There is no going back. Forget that. The children's bedrooms and another bathroom. But after only a moment we know the inevitable now and I take off my shoes and start to ascend stair by stair, arms held out as though I could make myself weightless. It would be a neat trick were it true, but, really, it's just a trick of the light. You look down at your feet. A trick played on your eye. You take off your shoes and start to ascend the exact same way.

You know how girls are, and this really is their domain, the parents don't even really get to come up here, hardly, the mother sometimes, and they're the girls' parents. But I beckon you on, as though I know there is something up here that I have to show you, and you follow on knowing that there is something here I will show you that you have to see.

Come a little closer. Listen. Stand there. Listen. You take up a position by the barely opened door of Sophie's bedroom. Liv has listened out for Julia wakening as the house cools down, realising she is in Sophie's bed and making her way downstairs, still essentially asleep, into her own bed. Liv has waited a few moments, listening as Julia settled, then she crept through to Sophie's bed, on tiptoes, more because the floor is now cold than to be as silent as she can be. Liv would leave it till the morning but what has happened is probably a big one, important, dangerous. So she has gently shaken Sophie awake, that'll do the trick, and then let her lie for a while.

It's time for us to take our chance. To find out what we need to know. Search the older girl. Yes, we need to know. OK, start with... open that drawer, look in there. That wardrobe, look through everything, the clothes she has hanging in there. Go through everything. I don't know, but we need to know. We'll know what we're looking for when we find it, so we have to go through everything. In the bottom of the wardrobe? Two rucksacks. OK. Dirty laundry? Are you sure? Clean. Clean laundry. OK. Do you think, one for the little girl and one for the older one? Preparation? Any money in there? Check, search through, pull the items of clothes, shake them loose item by item. Because we need to know. I don't know, money, maybe. We can't know until we know. Any money? Any money? I don't care about feelings of violation. Check. Then double check. Money would be the giveaway. That they're planning something. I do not care about your reservations. I do not even care about your feelings. This is what we need to know. Because we need to. OK. That chest of drawers. All the drawers. Yes, the knickers drawer. Do I have to repeat over and over? Because we need to know. Because that's why we're here. See? Yes, two fifties, two twenties and a bunch of tens is significant. What would a young girl like this need with this money? Well, OK, holiday money, Christmas money, gifts money. But it's suspicious. We have to be suspicious. Because we have to. OK. The girl. No, not her. The older girl. Oh, save your horror. We need to know. I told you I do not care about your reservations. This is the story. This is how the story ends. This is how the story has to end. I don't care. I don't care. This is how we get to know what's going on. By searching, yes, by finding, yes, by being suspicious, yes. Now, search the girl. Go on. Search her. Search her. Across there. Yes. Underneath. Yes. Along her arms. Because we need to know. Necessity. This is what is necessary. The need to know. The need to complete the story. To see all, hear all, understand all. Search up along her left leg. Go on. Search down along her right leg. It doesn't matter about violation. It's what's needed. I told you. Necessity. Knowing the story. Check the socks. The bra. Go on. Check them. Check them! Feel along her collar, her cuffs, her waistband, where the material is thicker. No, I won't ask you to do that. But we need you to search her down there. Yes. Yes. Yes. We need to know. Search her. Search. Down there. Check. Search. Show me. A fifty. See. Her keeping it down there. Now that's hiding it, isn't it? That's suspicious. What does a teenage girl need with a fifty down her knickers? She's planning a runaway. No? Yes. What does she need with money on her, there? Eh. Oh, spare me your disgust. We got the information we needed, didn't we? That was a low trick, was it? Maybe so. That was a dirty trick? I accept that. Forgive me. I'm terribly sorry. Nah, you can leave the other one.

Coming awake, Liv thinks, so she can explain, so Sophie can take in what she has to be told.

'Tell me again.'

'Oh, Liv, I've told you I'm sorry.'

'OK. It's OK. I understand. I just need to know what happened. Everything you can remember about it.'

'It was today.'

'Definitely today?'

'Yes. It was today. And they went missing.'

'I told you to delete everything immediately.'

'I can't keep track that way. Of what I've said. Of what other people have said.'

'We have to. It's not just a… It's people getting into our phones and taking the data away. I told you all this stuff already. People want our data. They want to harm us, hurt us.'

'I'm sorry, Liv.'

'OK. OK. It's not your fault. OK. How many messages?'

'Ten. Maybe twenty.'

'That means thirty at least, then. Maybe fifty.'

'Liv!'

'OK. Sorry. OK.'

'I didn't mean it.'

'I've told you before, you have to delete all texts as soon as you send them. Or receive them.'

'I kept losing track of what I've said. I'm sorry. I'm sorry, Liv.'

'It's just. It's just, we have to be safe. Do you understand?'

'Yes.'

'Do you?'

'Yes, I understand, Liv. Please don't shout. Please.'

'I have to keep you safe. Do you understand?'

'Yes. You're scaring me.'

'We need to be scared. No one's going to help us. But I'll be with you. We have to do it.'

'Yes, Liv. I do understand.'

'I know you do. I know. We have to be patient. Look, I'm sorry. I don't mean we have to be scared. We just— We just have to be safe. I want you to be safe. Do you understand?'

'Yes.'

'I know you do. I'm sorry.'

'No, I'm sorry.'

'OK. We're both sorry. We're both very, very sorry. When it's not us that have anything to be sorry about.'

'No.'

'No.'

'Liv?'

'God. I am really sorry, Sophie.'

'Liv?'

'What?'

'Are there people going to, I don't know, come for us one day? Kidnap us or something?'

'I shouldn't think so. You have nothing to be worried about, at least on that front.'

'You're sure?'

'Yes.'

'Really sure?'

'Yes. What's making you think that?'

'Well, it's just, well, basically, people go missing, don't they?'

'Some people go missing from their lives, Sophie, yes. It doesn't always mean they've been kidnapped.'

'Yes, but women. Women and girls, basically they go missing sometimes and they have been kidnapped.'

'Sometimes, OK, I admit. But that's extremely rare.'

'Yes, but that girl, the little girl with the eye, the little thing in her eye, the one we've to look out for.'

'Yes, but she was just a tiny little girl, Sophie.'

'Yes, but women go missing too. They literally do.'

'Very rarely, Sophie. I'm not sure…'

'But they do.'

'They do, but…'

'That university lady. She was just going to her job, at the university.'

Liv looks at her sister, who is looking at her.

'No one's coming for us, Sophie.'

'It's just, you know, that Milly girl. Didn't she get taken away eventually? Literally kidnapped. Killed or something. And that was because her phone was hacked.'

'Oh, Sophie. You've got it a bit the wrong way round. Milly's phone was hacked *because* she was kidnapped and killed, she wasn't killed because she was hacked.'

'Oh.'

'Sophie. Come here. Don't worry, we're safe. I'll make us safe.'

'And Mum and Dad?'

'I've told you. I'll make you safe.'

'But what about Mum and Dad?'

'We have to look after us.'

'Not Mum and Dad?' Sophie says.

'Those two?' Liv says.

We look across at each other, hearing, looking. You and I, watching, listening. Don't lower your eyes. See everything.

'That pair are not to be trusted.'

---

* Characters' first names in this book have been changed from their actual character names to protect the identities of these characters in this book.

† This character's first name in this book was probably falsified by the character in order to obscure his identity from another character in this book.